SOMETHING FORBIDDEN

FUNERALS AND WEDDINGS ~ BOOK FOUR

BERNADETTE MARIE

5 PRINCE PUBLISHING

Published by 5 PRINCE PUBLISHING & BOOKS, LLC

PO Box 865, Arvada, CO 80001

www.5PrinceBooks.com

ISBN digital: 978-1-63112-270-5

ISBN print: 978-1-63112-271-2

Cover Credit: Marianne Nowicki

To Stan,
I can't imagine that anything would have kept me from falling in love
with you.

ACKNOWLEDGMENTS

To my boys: I hope that you will always have each other's backs the way the *Fab Five* do in this series. I love the bond that you share, and seeing you all together (often) makes me happy.

To Mom and Sissy: I'm always grateful to have you near to support me in all my crazy endeavors.

To Cate: I can't imagine what I did right to align our stars (even though we walked the same halls for years). Thank you for always making me look good.

To my *Book Hive*, my Street Team, my Beta Readers, and my Readers who love HEA: Thank you from the bottom of my heart for loving the *Fab Five*, embracing their struggles, and supporting their normalizing of mental health care. I love to write for you all.

ALSO BY BERNADETTE MARIE

THE KELLER FAMILY SERIES

The Executive's Decision

A Second Chance

Opposite Attraction

Center Stage

Lost and Found

Love Songs

Home Run

The Acceptance

The Merger

The Escape Clause

A Romance for Christmas

THE WALKER FAMILY SERIES

Walker Pride

Stargazing

Walker Bride

Wanderlust

Walker Revenge

Victory

Walker Spirit

Beginnings

Walker Defense

Masterpiece

At Last

THE MATCHMAKER SERIES

Matchmakers

Encore

Finding Hope

THE THREE MRS. MONROES TRILOGY

Amelia

Penelope

Vivian

THE ASPEN CREEK SERIES

First Kiss

Unexpected Admirer

On Thin Ice

Indomitable Spirit

THE DENVER BRIDE SERIES

Cart Before the Horse

Never Saw it Coming

Candy Kisses

ROMANTIC SUSPENSE

Chasing Shadows

PARANORMAL ROMANCES

The Tea Shop

The Last Goodbye

HOLIDAY FAVORITES

Corporate Christmas

Tropical Christmas

Date for Hire

THE DEVEREAUX FAMILY SERIES

Kennedy Devereaux

Chase Devereaux

Max Devereaux

Paige Devereaux

FUNERALS AND WEDDINGS SERIES

Something Lost

Something Discovered

Something Found

Something Forbidden

Something New

SOMETHING FORBIDDEN

CHAPTER 1

*N*oises from upstairs had Sarah staring at the ceiling. Her head pounded from the amount of wine she'd had to drink at Kelly and Ray's wedding, and the lack of sleep she'd gotten after that.

An arm was draped over her, and there was a soft snore coming from the man next to her. She turned her head to see Bruce with a content smile, even in sleep. What in the hell had they done?

Oh, she knew what she'd done. She'd played out that scenario in her head a million and one times since she was a teenager. But, God, she wasn't a teenager anymore. Bruce was her brother's best friend. She'd known the man, whose bare leg brushed up against hers, since she was five.

And since she was five, her brother Alex had warned her to stay away from Bruce, and vice versa. Well, she could officially say that neither of them had heeded the warnings, and now here they were—naked, and in the basement apartment of her brother's house.

"You are thinking way too hard when you should be sleeping,"

Bruce's voice broke through the silence, though only a whisper dipped in sleep.

"They're up," she whispered. "We were going to be out of here before they got up."

"It's five-thirty in the morning. They have an infant. It always sounds like that up there."

Sarah rolled toward him. "How in the hell are we going to get me out of here?"

"Wait until you hear running water, then you'll know they're in the shower."

She snorted a quiet laugh. "They shower together? One of them will be up."

He shook his head, rustling his mussed hair against the pillow. "They do, in fact, shower together. It saves time and money, he says. They can also put the baby in her seat while they shower real fast, and sometimes they take her in with them so they don't have to do the whole bath thing."

"You have a lot of information."

"These walls aren't as thick as they should be. But it's freaking cheap to live here, so here I am. Besides, they'll leave early for basketball at the Y. They stop for donuts on Sundays."

She'd lost track of the day, she decided, and let her body relax against the bed.

"I play with you guys every week. I never get donuts."

Bruce chuckled. "I'll get you donuts. I'll get you anything you could ever want."

"I want him not to kill us."

Bruce shrugged.

Yeah, they were screwed.

The timing of all of this sucked. Sarah had moved back home with her mother while her new townhouse was being built. She wasn't in any better a situation than Bruce was. She might not be a teenager anymore, but she was going to have to sneak around like one if she was going to enjoy his company.

So, there they would hide, in Bruce's basement apartment with her brother living his life upstairs with his wife and daughter.

"Why didn't you move into Catherine's place when she moved in here?" she whispered, which she'd been doing all night.

"Too much money. Remember, I was broke and desolate when I moved in here when Craig owned it. Things have only slightly gotten better in the financial department."

"Toby doesn't pay you well?" She teased, referring to the job another one of his best friends had given him in his high tech business.

He chuckled softly. "I'm paid well. But I have to build a nest egg back up to get on my feet."

Okay, she understood that, but at that moment she wished he'd moved into Catherine's old place.

"He's going to kill us," she said and Bruce tightened his arm around her.

"It would be totally worth it," he grinned again, his eyes still closed.

"We're going to have to talk about this."

"I'm sure we will."

"You're not taking this very seriously, are you?"

His eyes opened slowly. "Sweetheart, you have no idea how seriously I'm taking this. I'm enjoying every single second of you being right here. Let me enjoy it."

Footsteps above them had her gripping the sheet around her. God, why hadn't they gone to a hotel? Because all of her money was tied up in her new house and Bruce was a bit down on his luck, as he'd reminded her.

Not that there would ever be a good time for them to be together, but now certainly wasn't it.

Everything between them had changed on New Year's Eve thanks to a little too much alcohol.

Since they'd been teenagers, they'd flirted, and tossed it

3

around in front of Alex to make him mad. But they both understood the situation. Anything between them was forbidden, because Alex said so.

Then again, who the hell was he to say they couldn't be together?

On New Year's Eve, they'd consumed enough alcohol, and mixed among the crowd, in Toby's enormous house, and they'd kissed. Years and years of pent up lust had broken free that night.

Thinking about that kiss still made her insides sizzle. Who knows where it might have ended had Ray not stopped them before Alex walked into the room?

Now, one wedding reception and plied with more alcohol, look where they'd landed.

Bruce's hand slid under the sheet and over her stomach. "You're thinking too much again."

"I can't help it."

"He never comes down here. Don't worry."

"I am worried."

"I know. So you'd better be very quiet," he said as he rolled himself on top of her.

"Not now that they're awake," she argued. Even as she did, she wrapped her arms around his neck.

"They were awake last night, too. We were just very quiet."

"He's going to kill us," she repeated.

Bruce lowered his mouth to hers. "No, he's only going to kill me. But we'll see how long we can go until he does."

When he kissed her, all of the common sense fell out of her head, again. She'd been chasing this moment all her life. There hadn't been a day that she hadn't had a crush on Bruce Griffin, but she'd known all along nothing would come of it.

CHAPTER 2

Bruce had been right. The shower had turned on and she could distinctly hear her brother and sister-in-law talking above them. The words were muffled, but they got in the shower and less than ten minutes later the water turned off.

Okay, Sarah was impressed. They were efficient. Still wrapped in Bruce's arms, she heard the little family upstairs pack up and head out the back door.

"Now we can rise," he said before he pressed a kiss to her neck.

"This was risky."

"It all was risky. We knew that going in."

Sarah turned to him. "Did we think about it though? I mean, I don't regret it, so don't think that I do, but we can't be doing this."

The crease that formed between Bruce's brows when he was thinking appeared. "I've waited my entire life for this moment, and you're going to just dismiss it?"

"You've waited for this?" She found that hard to believe.

"You're oblivious to this?"

"To what?"

Bruce propped himself up on his elbow and looked down at her. "I've been chasing you my whole life. I mean seriously. Okay, when we were little, you were just the cute little sister. But, think back. When Alex would send you away, I protested. I didn't mind you around. When you grew up, then my attention was on you—always you."

She blinked hard. "I thought you just messed with me to get to Alex."

"I did. But that's why he'd get so worked up. Everyone knows how I feel about you. I figured you didn't feel the same for me, so why bother."

"Okay, this is a lot to take in."

Bruce laid back and laughed as he rubbed his chest. "Well, I've just confessed one of my biggest secrets to you, except that I love you. So when your brother kills me…"

"You love me?"

Bruce turned his head and their eyes locked again. "Sweetheart, my heart has never belonged to anyone else."

Sarah sat up, the sheet wrapped around her as if to save face. She sucked in a breath, and then another.

Bruce sat up and took the bottle of water from the night stand and handed it to her. "You're freaking me out," he said as he watched her drink. "Why does any of this surprise you?"

How much should she tell him? Hell, he'd just confessed a life time of feelings for her, she'd be an idiot not to reciprocate.

Sarah swallowed down the warm water, and then twisted the lid back on the bottle. She took one more moment to think about what she was going to say as she set the bottle on the table next to her.

"I thought you were just always nice to me," she admitted.

"Well, at least you thought I was nice." He ran his hand down her arm. "Everyone knows how I feel."

"The truth is, I've always felt that way about you, too."

She watched as his eyes went wide. "I'm thirty-three years old living in your brother's basement. I'm oblivious to most things. But I didn't know you felt that way. I thought you just went along with me to tease your brother."

"It was a bonus, but you've always stirred me up."

Bruce laughed, and they weren't quiet now. "Shit. Well, shit," he repeated. "Here we are sneaking around, and we should have been together this whole time. How dumb are we?"

"We still can't just jump out of bed and head out and tell him."

"Why not?"

Sarah shrugged. "Why doesn't he want us together? I mean that's the perfect romance trope, right?"

"Trope?"

"Yeah, best friend falls in love with the little sister? Never heard of it?"

"I don't stick my nose in romance novels or rom coms, thank you very much."

Sarah laughed. "That's bullshit. I know you have a thing for Sandra Bullock movies."

"Can't help it."

"We have to keep this low profile for the moment. I don't want to set him off right now. There's too much at stake."

"Such as?"

"Your living arrangement for one."

Bruce nodded. "Right." He took her hand and pulled her on top of him.

Sarah straddled him, running her hands over his chest. "Do you really love me?" she asked as he ran his hands over her thighs.

"I can honestly say I do. And, you know I'm not saying it because the sex is incredible."

"No one has ever said they love me before. Well, no man has ever said it."

7

"I find that hard to believe. I happen to know how many men you've been with."

Sarah winced. "What a horrible way to start something new. Maybe you know me too well."

"We still have secrets."

"I don't have too many."

"I don't hold anything you've ever done against you," he said as his hands skimmed up her sides. "I'd hope you feel the same way."

Sarah puckered her lips. "Mindy Martin. Julie Fitzpatrick. Carmen DeSanta. Olivia Miller. Samantha—"

Bruce put his hand over her mouth. "You're ruining this very special moment."

"You're telling me they didn't mean anything?"

He chewed his bottom lip. "I almost asked Mindy Martin to marry me."

They were being candid, but Sarah didn't like what it did to her insides when he said it out loud. "I didn't realize you guys were that serious. Was that during the time I was away at college?"

"Yeah." Bruce ran his hands over her shoulders and down her arms. "We were good together. Then she got a job in Florida, and I needed to stay here."

"Why?"

"It's how I was programmed."

And in the moment Bruce said that, she wondered if that was some of the reason Alex had always forbidden her to have anything to do with him. There was a side to Bruce that no one ever saw, but they'd been around him long enough to know it.

"Maybe you should have gone and gotten away from here," she offered.

The flash of sadness in his eyes told her he'd thought about that too. "We should get going." He sat up and wrapped his arms around her while she still straddled him. "You always pick me for your team. Are you going to pick me today?"

Sarah cupped Bruce's face, which was now marred with an underlying sadness. "I will never not pick you," she promised, and she hoped he understood the real meaning behind it.

CHAPTER 3

*B*ruce had driven Sarah to her car, and headed to the YMCA. He pulled up and parked next to Alex who was taking Celia Rose out of her car seat.

"Where's your wife?" Bruce asked, noticing that Catherine wasn't around.

"She ran inside to pee," he laughed. "The baby is heavy on her bladder today."

Bruce nodded thinking that was too much information. He opened the back of his car and took out his gym bag as Alex moved toward him, the sleeping baby resting on his shoulder.

"Had some company last night, huh?" Alex winked.

Bruce was sure he'd felt the blood drain from his face. "What makes you say that?"

"Walls are thin, my friend."

There was a pain in his gut now. "I didn't mean to make any noise."

"I just heard whispering, that's all. Who was it?"

Oh hell no! He wasn't going there right now, though it would be the right time, he figured. Alex wasn't going to punch him, or kill him, with his daughter in his arms.

"Don't worry about it."

Alex shook his head. "Always the playboy. Think you'll ever settle down? You can't just bring home women for the rest of your life."

Now that he'd landed the only woman he'd ever wanted, he didn't want to take another woman to bed—ever.

"Let's just not worry about my sex life."

Alex studied him as they started to walk toward the front door. "Everything okay? Last night didn't go as you'd expected?"

"It went better than expected. I just have a lot on my mind, that's all."

Celia Rose lifted her head and looked at her father, and then at Bruce. She smiled at him before she rested her tired head back to Alex's shoulder.

Bruce envied what Alex had. Married with a daughter and another on the way. He was one lucky bastard. And didn't it mar the perfect image when Alex said things like 'always the playboy' to Bruce, insinuating that he'd never have what Alex had. Then again, Bruce knew he'd never have what Alex had. It wasn't in the cards.

"Hey, losers!" Sarah's voice rang out from behind them.

They both stopped and turned. Celia Rose perked up at the sight of her aunt and held her arms out.

Sarah carried a box of donuts, which she handed to Bruce before taking the baby from her brother. "There's my girl," she said as she nuzzled her nose into her niece's neck. "I missed you."

"You saw her yesterday," Alex reminded her.

"Yeah, but she loves me the most so I miss her." Sarah walked past them and toward the door, her gym bag hanging from her shoulder. "I brought donuts because I was informed you get them before the game but never bring extras. So I'm sharing with everyone but you," she said to her as she walked to the court acting exactly as she would any other Sunday morning.

"God, she's a snot," Alex said as he laughed. But when he

turned back toward Bruce, who knew he wore worry on his face by the way that Alex looked at him, he stopped. "Seriously, what happened last night? You were fine at the wedding, and today you're out of sorts."

Bruce balanced the box in his hand and took a breath. "Mindy Martin."

"That's a name from the past. Was that who you had in bed with you?"

"No. What? No. She's married and lives across the country."

"So why bring her up?"

"Should I have married her and moved away all those years ago?"

Alex's eyes had gone wide. "What is this about?"

"Just something that came up in conversation. What if I'd gotten out of here when I could have?"

Alex blew out a breath. "You never would have. You wouldn't have left your grandparents. Do you have an opportunity?"

He'd like to think he did. "It's just heavy on my mind. I'm the son of some deranged serial killer who was hidden here with his grandparents. What if I left? Would it all come back to haunt me?"

The look on Alex's face was one of pure shock. Bruce was sure he'd even choked on his breath as he lifted his hand to rest it on Bruce's arm.

Alex stood silent for a moment studying him, concern masking his face. "Damn. You should talk to Rachel. Get some help."

Bruce snorted. "I've been in counseling my whole life. You know that."

"I do. And in fifteen years, I haven't heard you talk about any of this, except that one time when you confided in me about it. What's bringing it up now? What happened?" Alex's voice shook with concern.

"That woman I was with last night, she's the one I want to spend my life with."

Alex pulled his hand back, blinked hard, and then a smile formed on his lips. "That's great. A little deep for conversation on a Sunday morning, but great. Who the hell is it?"

"I'll tell you when I'm ready."

"You think she's going to bolt when you tell her all this personal stuff?"

"She knows I was raised by my grandparents because my dad is in jail and my mom died."

"She doesn't know the other details?"

"No." At least he didn't think she knew.

"You're afraid she'll look at you different?"

"I'm surprised she looked at me at all," he admitted. "I guess we'll see how it goes, huh?"

They started toward the court. "I'm here for ya, man. Whatever you need, you know I always have your back."

He did know that, but this was an exception, wasn't it?

And the moment they walked into the gym it hit him. Bruce knew exactly why Alex didn't want him to have anything to do with his sister. Had he been so oblivious to everything all this time? He'd thought for all those years it was because Sarah was the little sister, and Bruce was the best friend. Those two things didn't mix and usually had iffy results.

But Bruce's story wasn't like everyone else's. It wasn't that Alex knew he'd shoplifted cigarettes when they were twelve and drank his grandfather's whiskey. It wasn't that he knew how many women Bruce had been with either. The pot, the drinking, that one night in jail because he'd propositioned a seventeen-year-old in a bar because she had a fake ID, but they'd only held him until he sobered up. Alex knew it all.

Then there was the other part of Bruce's life. It was one thing to have a parent in jail and a parent dead. It was another to have the blood of some serial killer run through your veins, and only Alex knew that.

Well, shit. Had he compartmentalized that so deep that he never even considered it? Bruce didn't have an evil thought in his head—ever. He'd never even been in a fist fight—ever. He might have overdone the weed in his life just to stay calm, but his father's blood wasn't thick enough, as far as he was concerned to make him a bad person.

"You don't feel good, do you?" Alex asked as he turned back toward him. "You're pale as a ghost."

Bruce nodded. "Yeah. I think I'll go back home."

And with that, he handed Alex the box of donuts, turned away from the gym, and back to his car. He had some demons to face, and he'd had no idea that they were going to surface after the amazing night he'd had with the only woman he'd truly loved.

CHAPTER 4

Sarah handed her niece to her sister-in-law and then sat down next to them to put on her high tops.

Catherine nudged her with her elbow. "You looked like you were having a nice time at the wedding last night," she said with a smile.

"I had a great time."

"I didn't tell Alex, but I saw you sneak off and come back."

Sarah felt the blood drain from her face. "Oh, yeah?"

"Who'd you sneak off with?"

Was this a game, Sarah wondered? Did she know and she was just looking for a confession? Or had she just seen Sarah disappear.

"Can't tell you that. Top secret."

Catherine blew out a breath. "Ya know, when Rachel was pregnant she'd make me spill everything because she just needed the gossip." Catherine rubbed her slightly swollen belly. "I get that now. I want gossip."

"I want some gossip. Who has gossip?" Rachel sat down next to them.

Catherine tilted her head in Sarah's direction. "She snuck away from the reception last night and then came back."

"Ooooo," Rachel teased. "Who'd ya get? Ray's cousin? He's a looker."

"No."

Rachel bit down on her lip. "There was that guy Ray works with, the foreman." Sarah shook her head. "Kelly's cousin?"

"I'm not saying anything. I don't have any gossip for you. Did you ever consider I left to go to the bathroom?"

Both women shook their heads.

Catherine lifted her shoulders and let them drop. "I guess we'll never know."

And that was exactly how Sarah wanted it. If things worked out, they'd all know. But they were walking on a tightrope, and if Alex found out, they'd fall off of it. So she wasn't going to help their need for gossip.

When Alex walked through the door and right to them, setting the box of donuts on the bench next to his wife, Sarah shifted to look behind him.

"You're down a guy," she said, noting her brother's face.

"Bruce went home."

Now the donut that she'd taken from the box on her drive in swam in her stomach. "Went home? This is now a two on two since Ray is on his honeymoon?"

"Guess so," he said, but his mind was still occupied with it, she could tell.

"So why'd he ditch us?"

Alex shrugged, but there was more to it. "He said he didn't feel well. Hell, he didn't look well either."

That was a load of bullshit. He'd been just fine that morning, feeling her up in his bed.

"Maybe he ran off to be with whomever he brought home last night," Catherine said with a grin as she bounced Celia Rose on her knee. "There is gossip still to be had."

"He took someone home last night?" Rachel's voice rose in pitch and interest.

"I guess they were in a hurry. I don't know why they didn't go to her house," Catherine teased. "Our house isn't really the ideal place to bring someone."

"This is good gossip."

Sarah finished tying her shoes, stood, and walked away from the small group. Her brother had angst written all over his face, her sister-in-law was in a gossip fest with her best friend, and all over her, but they didn't know it.

What the hell was wrong with Bruce anyway? And what did Alex know? There wasn't any trash talk going on between him and Toby and Craig. He wasn't razzing her about sneaking away last night. Something had gone down in the parking lot between her brother and Bruce, that much she was sure of. Well she'd be damned if Bruce was going to play her like he played others. Sarah Burke wasn't an average woman. She was a kick ass one, and anyone could take that metaphorically or literally.

When Craig threw the ball in her direction, she caught it and made a basket from center court. All three men shook their heads.

Toby leaned his hands on his knees and looked up at her. "Maybe to make it fair, you could play all three of us. I mean, it'd give us a shot, sort of."

BRUCE SLAMMED THROUGH THE BACKDOOR OF THE HOUSE AND down the steps. Wasn't this the evil side effect of PTSD? It just freaking showed up whenever the hell it wanted to!

He supposed he was lucky. He could enjoy the Fourth of July, and Rachel hid after having been shot. But that was freaking luck and he knew it. There was no reason he shouldn't be affected by fireworks, backfiring cars, lightning, or doors slamming.

He paced circles around the pool table before plopping down on the couch and resting his head in his hands.

The speeding ticket he'd gotten on the way home hadn't helped his mood any. It was like the freaking cop was just waiting for him to happen by.

Bruce blew out a breath—and then another.

Okay, he needed to pull out his mental tool box and work through this shit that was riddling him with anxiety.

One of the things he'd always done was surround himself with supportive people. That was one of his first lessons when he was eleven, and the Burke family happened to be part of that process.

He and Alex had become fast friends that summer he moved in with his grandparents. He supposed he owed them a lot of credit for even letting him out of the house. Back then his original name and his picture had been splattered all over the news stations outside of Chicago after his father had been arrested. The boy who moved in with his grandparents was different.

They'd made sure to introduce him as Bruce Griffin, their grandson, even though they weren't biologically his grandparents. They'd been part of the foster system, and eventually adopted him. But they were never Mom and Dad.

Bruce shook his hands to bring the blood back to his fingers when he realized he been clenching his fists.

Alex was the only person in the entire world, next to his grandparents, that knew about his dad. But even Alex, the keeper of all his secrets, didn't know Bruce's real name.

CHAPTER 5

*A*fter forty-five minutes of half-assed basketball, they had decided to call the game. Without Ray and Bruce, it was worthless, and with the attitude Sarah and her brother had, well, it just wasn't a good time.

As a group, they all walked out to the parking lot. Toby went his way toward his BMW parked far away from the other cars. Rachel hugged both Catherine and Sarah, then split off with Craig and their daughter.

"Do you have dinner plans tonight?" Catherine asked Sarah as she took Celia Rose from Alex so that she could put her in her car seat.

Sarah chewed on her bottom lip. If she took the invitation, it would get her into the house, and maybe she could talk to Bruce. Then again, if he was running away from her, then she didn't want to be near him at all.

Or, he was just sick, and if she was at the house she could offer him help.

"Earth to Sarah," Catherine laughed as she opened the door to put their daughter in the car.

"Sorry. I guess I was trying to think through my day."

Catherine laughed. "I get that way. There are days that I think Ray has second thoughts about hiring me."

"I doubt that. What time for dinner?"

"Six?"

"What can I bring?"

Catherine gave it a moment of thought. "Dessert. But make it chocolate," she said with a smile before ducking into the car to fasten Celia Rose into the seat.

Sarah nodded, smiled at her brother and started toward her car. A moment later, she felt his presence, and when she looked behind her, Alex was following her.

"You know I'll kick anyone's ass that jumps me. You don't have to follow me to my car in the middle of a Sunday," she quipped as she pushed the button to unlock her car.

"Bruce didn't say anything to you this morning did he?"

Sarah felt her temperature rise, and wondered if it reached her cheeks. "What would he have said to me that he didn't say to you?" she asked, wondering if he knew she was the one in the basement with him.

"I guess you didn't talk to him much more than I did."

Okay, that was close. "No. What's wrong with him?"

Alex shrugged, tucked his hands into his pockets, and rocked back on his heels. "I don't know. He said something about Mindy Martin and how he should have married her and left town all those years ago. Then he went pale and took off."

Sarah bit down hard to keep her jaw from trembling. Was that what he said? Shit! So last night was a one and done, and he'd said all those nice things to her.

"Well, I guess he'd better go find Mindy Martin and get his shit in order."

Her brother's brows narrowed. "She's married. He just gets like this once in a while, and I don't blame him." He ran his hand over his hair. "I'll talk to him. He'll be fine soon."

"Why does he get like this?" she asked because she had to know.

"The same reason Rachel hides from fireworks. Stuff just sets him off."

"Like trauma?"

He actually winced. "Something like that."

"What did Mindy do to him? She really must have done a number on him," she said through gritted teeth as she gripped her car keys tighter to keep her hands from shaking.

Alex narrowed his eyes on her as if her demeanor was equally as odd as Bruce's had been. "Nah, I think it has something to do with family."

Sarah swallowed hard, perhaps grateful that it wasn't about Mindy Martin. "Does it have something to do with his dad being in jail?"

Alex puckered his lips. "I didn't know you knew that."

"I remember it from when we were little. He moved in with his grandparents after his mom died, and he couldn't live with his dad because he was in jail."

"You've carried that with you since you were little?"

Sarah shrugged. "Did you know anyone else whose mom had died? It stuck with me."

"And you know why he's in jail?"

"No. Do you?" she asked, wondering what kind of secrets her brother had.

He took a breath and let it out slowly. "No," he said firmly, though she wasn't sure she believed him. "I'll talk to him when I get home. See you at six?"

Now she wasn't sure she should show up. But this was her brother, and they were tight. And it meant she could spend more time with her niece. "Yes. I'll be there."

He gave her a smile and headed back to the car.

Sarah slid into her car and started the engine, but she didn't drive away. Instead, she began to cry. What the hell happened?

That morning, hiding in his bed, they had been fine. Hadn't he even told her he loved her and always had?

He wasn't sick. That much she knew.

What was she supposed to do? Should she call him? Text him? Just act like it was nothing and go to dinner and then home for the night?

And what was that all about Mindy Martin? Had she brought this on herself by mentioning the woman's name? Did he really still think he should have married her, even after he confessed to always having loved Sarah?

Or had Sarah just fallen for some shtick to get her into his bed?

That very thought made her blood pressure rise, even though she didn't really believe that was the case. There had always been a chemistry between her and Bruce. And she'd wanted last night so bad she'd made the first move.

~

BRUCE SAT WITH HIS LAPTOP ON THE SMALL TABLE IN HIS apartment. Staring at the screen, he didn't even recognize the face of the man he had once called Dad.

He ran his hand over his hair. Why had this hit him all of a sudden? What had brought it to the surface and made him say the words serial killer in conversation with Alex? It didn't need to be said. It had been said only once before, when he confessed his entire life to Alex at the age of seventeen. So why, after a night with the only woman he'd ever really loved, did he spiral into the abyss of what had happened to him when he was ten? In that year before he became Bruce Griffin, he'd overcome more than most people would in their entire life.

Therapy had always helped. The gift to compartmentalize his past from the present served him well. It was only in rare times like these that the life he'd curated mixed with the one he'd been born into.

He owed Sarah an apology for disappearing. God, he wished they each had their own place. Starting up whatever they were starting was hard enough when they intended to keep it from Alex. It was even harder when they had nowhere to go to be alone.

CHAPTER 6

*B*ruce heard the back door open and the family walk through. Looking at his watch, he figured he had exactly four minutes before Alex knocked on the basement wall to announce himself.

Closing his laptop, and tucking his past away again, he moved to the couch, turned on the TV and poised himself as if nothing else had been going on all day.

It took six minutes for Alex to appear at the bottom of the stairs.

"You doing okay, man?" he asked without crossing the threshold into the basement.

"Peachy keen, jelly bean," he replied as he changed the channel.

"Which means you're wallowing. Those are your code words, in case you didn't know."

Bruce laughed. "And that's why we've been best friends our entire life. You pick that shit up even when I don't."

Alex shrugged and walked into the room. He pulled one of the chairs away from the small table, turned it around, and straddled it, resting his arms on the back of it as he faced Bruce.

"Seriously, are you okay? All of that came from left field today."

Bruce muted the TV and set the remote on the coffee table. "I'm going to be okay. I don't know when it's going to surface and what form it'll take, but when it does, this is the path."

Alex nodded. "Can I say you do really well with it? In all these years, I've only seen it outwardly affect you a few times."

"I'm the same age my father was when they locked him up," he said. "I just read that in an article. I didn't know that."

"So it's not what set you off?"

Bruce shook his head. In order to talk this out, he had to give Alex a little information, but he wasn't going to out them. Hell, he didn't want to know if this was why Alex wanted him to stay away from Sarah.

"My overnight guest and I were having a heart to heart," he began, "and we stumbled over the names of women I'd had relationships with."

"That is never good pillow talk," Alex said with a chuckle.

"Obviously. But I admitted that I had considered proposing to Mindy."

"I don't think I knew that."

"You were already gone by then," Bruce reminded him. "You were on your East Coast adventure. I was trying to find my place among the adults."

"I should have stayed for you."

That made Bruce laugh. "I should have gone with you," he admitted. "But you were right. I never would have left my grandparents. I needed to stay right where I was planted."

"So, Mindy, huh?"

"At that moment, she was the one. Everything was always perfect with us. Weirdly perfect. It helped that my grandmother adored her. We had long talks about getting married and having kids. Then she got the job offer in Florida and I wouldn't even consider leaving."

"Why?"

Bruce looked him right in the eye. "What if I set up house somewhere else and someone figured out who I was?"

"You never told Mindy?"

"Nope. The person I was and my family before my grandparents didn't exist, as far as I was concerned."

"It could happen here too, you know. Someone could figure out who you are."

"I've considered that. But I feel safe here, among all of you."

Alex rubbed his hand over his chin. "But I'm the only person in this entire world, aside from your grandparents, that knows?"

And he didn't even know it all, Bruce thought. "Yeah." Bruce stood and paced a little circle near the couch. "Here's the thing. Much like after Rachel got shot and then the fireworks set her off, knowing that this woman means this much to me seems to have brought this to the surface. It comes on fast and it comes in hot."

"And this is why you always have a revolving door of women? You can't get too close to just one?"

"Let's assume that's the case. I told this one I loved her. Mindy is the only other woman I have told that to."

"And you went through this then. too?"

"Silently and alone," he admitted. "I want to let you know it's going to need more processing now."

Alex nodded. "Okay, what does that mean?"

"It means this morning when I blurted out the words to you, it startled me. I didn't know it was going to surface like that. It just came out. But when I came home, I dragged out my laptop and looked up the stories."

Alex winced. "Why would you do that?"

"To torture myself," he admitted. "But they're doing some biographical TV thing on people like my father," he said without using the words. "It's been twenty-two years since they locked him up. I guess people want to rehash this shit."

"I'm so sorry, man. I'll cancel the TV account."

That made Bruce laugh. "I'm just telling you because I saw it was out there. I don't assume that anyone will watch it and associate me with it."

"What if they say your name?"

Bruce tucked his hands in his pockets and rocked back on his heels. "Let's just say I stand before you today with a name used to protect the innocent."

Alex stood from his chair. "Bruce Griffin isn't your name?"

"Sure it is. Legally."

"But it wasn't your given name."

"Right. That person is dead."

"You're not going to get in trouble by telling me that, right?"

Bruce chuckled. "No. I live in the same house with your family. I owe you the courtesy of being honest with you. You know who I am. You know me better than anyone else on this planet, including my grandmother."

"I don't think you're him, for the record."

"You don't know how much that means to me, sincerely."

"You're going to talk to someone about this though, right? I mean, you don't deserve to have this come up and wreck your life every time you fall in love."

Bruce smiled. "I'll call my therapist first thing in the morning."

"We can call Rachel if we have to."

"She doesn't need this part of me. She has her own healing to do. And you don't need to worry about me either. I'm not homicidal or suicidal. A little mopey for a moment, but I don't want to take you away from your family and your new baby worrying about me."

"You're my brother."

"I appreciate that, too. Your family has always accepted me, and that brought a lot of healing to me when I was younger."

"I'm glad we were there for you." Alex moved to him and

pulled him in. "I mean it when I say you're my brother. I will always be here for you."

And Bruce wondered just how true that was. "Thank you."

Alex stepped back. "Are you around tonight?"

"Yeah. I don't have any plans."

"Good. Sarah is coming over for dinner. Come up and join us."

The invitation hit Bruce right in the chest. She was coming to the house. He needed to put this behind him and quick. There couldn't be any awkwardness between them.

"I'll do that," he said.

Alex smiled and walked back up the stairs.

Bruce fell back to the couch. He needed to push this out of his head, and quick. The task of compartmentalizing it just as he always did needed to happen immediately, and he was trained in making that happen. He absolutely didn't want to risk losing Alex or Sarah. His intentions were pure. He did want to have Sarah in his life forever, only now as his lover and if he could manage it, in his twisted world of secrets, his wife.

CHAPTER 7

*S*arah had started a text to her brother four times to tell him she needed a raincheck. That was until she realized they'd extended the invitation for dinner to her mother as well.

"I'll just ride over with you tonight," she'd said in casual conversation.

Perhaps that was better. She couldn't linger uncomfortably hoping to get a moment to talk to Bruce if her mother was going to want to get home.

Because she was curious, in her own right, she sat down with her laptop and googled Mindy Martin. Of course the search turned up thousands of them. But, Sarah knew enough to narrow it down until she found her.

Mindy and Bruce had gone to high school together, and if Sarah remembered correctly, they'd gone out a few times when Bruce was in college. She couldn't hold his relationship with Mindy over him, she thought.

Sarah was six years younger than Bruce and her brother. By the time they were out of college, she was finishing high school. Alex headed off to the East Coast, and Bruce went on with his life, occasionally stopping in to say hello to her and her parents.

She would have just been little sister material still back then.

There was that one winter break when she was home from college, though, she remembered. Why hadn't that crossed her mind instead of Mindy Martin?

Bruce had dropped by at Thanksgiving when she'd been home. It wasn't out of the ordinary. Bruce had always been a staple in their home. Her dad had invited him in, and it was a year that Alex hadn't come home, but Bruce still dropped by.

When he'd learned that she'd be back for winter break, he showed up the first night Sarah was home. They'd gone out for pizza and played basketball in the driveway until her father had turned the lights out on them.

Bruce had come back each night, after dinner, and they did the same, sometimes even shoveling the snow off the drive.

Had he loved her then?

He was just an older brother to her, but she'd been smitten. There had always been something about Bruce that stirred her up.

She smiled as she looked at the Facebook photo of Mindy Martin, her husband, and three kids at Disneyland. Thank goodness it hadn't worked out between her and Bruce.

"Who is that?" her mother's voice came from behind her.

"An old girlfriend of Bruce's. We were talking about her and I was just curious about what she was up to."

Her mother sat down across from her with a cup of tea. "How is Bruce? I didn't talk to him at Alex and Catherine's reception. And I don't think I've seen him since."

"He was at Ray and Kelly's wedding."

Her mother puckered her lips in thought. "I guess I didn't notice."

And that was probably for the better, Sarah thought. She wasn't sure just how discreet they had been.

"He's doing okay. He's working for Toby and trying to save

enough to move out of Alex's basement. But with the housing market the way it is…"

"I think it's a terrible time for you to build that house of yours when you're perfectly welcome to live here as long as you like."

Sarah pushed a smile to her lips. They'd had this conversation more than she'd have liked.

"I do appreciate that, Mom. But I want to have my own. I'm twenty-six, and I work hard."

Her mother nodded. "I know. It's selfish of me. Maybe I just need to meet someone."

When her mother said things like that, Sarah wanted to protest. But the truth was, her father had been gone almost five years. Her mother had a lot of life left, and she was obviously lonely.

"And where are you going to meet someone?"

Her mother shrugged. "On the pickle ball court, or maybe in a water aerobics class," she laughed. "Don't any of your friends have single dads?"

Sarah wanted to laugh, but her mother appeared to be very serious. "I don't know."

"Well," she lifted her tea cup to her mouth and blew. "It'll happen if it's supposed to happen. For you, too," she added. "There will be someone that comes along for you."

"Who said I was looking?"

"Oh, you should look, honey. You're young, fit, beautiful, successful. You deserve a man who sees all those things."

It was dangerous, but Sarah thought she'd dip into the conversation more. "What if I told you I found someone like that."

Her mother narrowed her gaze at her. "I'd say you're still feeling it out. I know you better than that. You'd have brought him home and introduced him to me."

Nope, she wasn't going to go further than that. Her mother knew Bruce as well as she did, though her mother might not have been able to name all the women he'd been with as Sarah had that morning.

"Maybe I should pool my resources with Bruce and we could both get out," she said lightly trying to ease the mood.

"Oh, Sarah, that's just silly," her mother laughed as she sipped her tea. "Alex wouldn't have that."

"It's not Alex's decision."

"But Bruce, really? He's like a brother to you."

"He's a man, Mom."

"Not one you marry."

Sarah closed her laptop. "Why not?"

"Why are you being so strange?"

"I'm not. I just happen to think Bruce is a great guy."

Her mother nodded. "I agree."

"So why wouldn't he be a good roommate?"

Her mother set down her mug. "I'm just saying I think Alex would have a problem with it."

"I don't."

"Then I guess that's good?" Her mother's lips pursed. "You do remember that he was raised by his grandparents because his father was in jail, don't you?"

"And that has what to do with the man who lives in the basement of your son's house where your granddaughter lives?"

The adjusted expression on her mother's face said she'd never thought of it that way. "How far does the apple fall from the tree?"

"Considering he's lived here, among all of us for twenty plus years as a model citizen, I would think that tree didn't have much to do with the fruit it bore."

"You're awfully defensive over him."

She supposed she was. "Sorry. I just happen to think he's a really great guy."

"He is, sweetheart. And maybe it would be good if you had a

roommate," she added. "I'd feel better about you being with someone in that house that you're building."

Sarah felt the corner of her mouth tug into a smile. Maybe there was a whole new deck of cards she could play. Wouldn't that make Alex squirm if she invited Bruce to live with her when her place was done? They wouldn't have to sneak around then.

The temperature in her body rose until she felt the bead of sweat under her ponytail run down her neck.

Oh this had just turned into a game of wit and will, she thought. She wanted Bruce. Okay, she'd had him, but she wanted this victory. Alex was just going to have to get used to it. Now, just to get Bruce alone long enough that they could discuss it, and she could figure out what the hell had happened to him after they'd crawled out of his bed.

CHAPTER 8

The doorbell rang and Bruce heard the scurry of feet over the floor above him. Muffled voices drifted through the vents and down the stairs. She was there.

He sucked in a breath, and then another. For the minute they were together that morning, they'd been perfectly normal together. They could do it again. After all, they'd fallen right into place after they'd made out on New Year's. That had had to last him nearly four months. The sex might have to last him a year before he'd get another shot, he had to think along those lines.

Toby had given all his employees a new bottle of the tequila he'd bought into, so Bruce thought he'd take that as his offering. Maybe it would take the edge off of all of them—well, everyone but Catherine.

When he walked up the stairs and turned the corner, it was Alex and Sarah's mother he saw first.

"Hello, Mrs. Burke," he said as he moved to her and kissed her cheek.

"Bruce, how are you?"

"I'm good. I'm really good," he said and he noticed Alex

watching him. "I'm good," he said again to ward off Alex's caution.

"You look good. Are you working out?"

He laughed. "Toby recently put in a state of the art gym at the office headquarters. I have been taking advantage of that."

"I want to get in on that," Sarah said as she walked into the kitchen and their eyes met.

He wanted to scoop her up and plant a kiss on that soft mouth, but he grinned, just as he would had they not been sleeping together.

"I can get you an interview and put in a good word for you," he offered.

"I'm happy to bribe Toby, though I can't imagine there is anything I could offer that he just couldn't buy for himself," she teased. "I guess I'll keep my YMCA membership." She walked into the kitchen, elbowed her brother in the side, and set her dessert down. "Where's my baby?"

Alex shook his head. "Catherine was just changing her."

"Auntie needs some snuggles," she said as she left the room again.

Whenever she'd breeze into a room it always stirred Bruce up, and now that seemed to be a heightened sensation. What he wouldn't give for some time alone with her...

A moment later Sarah poked her head back into the kitchen. "How long before dinner?"

"Twenty minutes. Why?" Alex asked.

"Catherine just mentioned that Celia Rose is going to need more diaper wipes. And though it could wait until tomorrow, it's what I can do to help out your beautiful wife. I'm going to run to the store. Need anything else?"

Alex shook his head. "I don't think so."

Before she turned, she bore a stare into Bruce.

"I'll ride with you. I want some soda for my fridge in the

basement," he said and followed her out of the house and to the car.

They took it coolly, just as they would have a few months ago.

Sarah unlocked her car and they each climbed in. She started the engine, and drove down the street. When she made her turn at the stop sign, she reached for his hand.

"I missed you today," she said without looking at him.

"I'm sorry about this morning," he confessed. "In the moment, I just couldn't seem to handle it."

"What it?"

"Everything it." He lifted her fingers to his lips and pressed a kiss to them. "Sometimes parts of my past come back at me and slap me hard," he admitted. "It just happens."

Sarah chewed her bottom lip. "Alex said you were sorry you didn't marry Mindy Martin."

Bruce closed his eyes and let out a breath. "I don't think that's what I said to him. I'm sorry that's what he said."

"Are you sorry you didn't marry Mindy Martin?"

"Not in the least."

Sarah pulled into the parking lot of the store, parked the car, and turned to him. "What did us sleeping together have to do with putting you in that mood that made you take off?"

"Who said it had anything to do with us sleeping together?"

"I say. I know we have to skirt around Alex for a little while. Are you going to be able to do it?"

"Are you going to still want to?"

"Don't keep talking in circles," she warned and her voice had lowered. "You said some very important things to me this morning, and I think we need to discuss that and feel this out."

"You're right."

"So, are you in love with me, or was I a conquest to you?"

He felt his mouth drop open. "Is that what you think?"

"Are you going to talk in circles all night long? Because it's pissing me off."

Bruce eased back in his seat. "I've always been in love with you."

"Since when?"

Bruce gave it some thought. There were years he loved the little sister, because he didn't have one. Then there were years he loved the sassy young lady, but it was innocent, she just made him happy. "I think I fell for you that winter you were home from college for winter break and we'd play basketball until your dad turned off the lights, and then we'd sit on the step until we were so frozen we couldn't talk anymore."

The anger she wore softened. "I was thinking about that today."

"We have a lot of history."

"We changed all of it when we walked down the stairs to your place last night," she admitted. "So, what do we do now?"

"I don't want to let that go. I don't want it to be a one night thing. I also know we can't bring it up right now."

Sarah nodded slowly. "I'm supposed to close on my house in six weeks."

"That's pretty exciting."

"I want you to move in with me."

The air stuck in his lungs when he took a breath. "Really?"

"I even told my mom it made sense."

"You told your mom about us?"

She shook her head. "No. I just said it would make sense if we moved in together. You'd get out of the basement. I'd have a roommate and that would make her feel at ease."

"I wouldn't be able to keep my hands off of you," he admitted.

Smiling, Sarah pushed herself out of her seat, over the center console, and straddled him in his seat. "I'd be disappointed if you tried."

Bruce gripped her hips and she dipped her mouth to take his. Her hands moved into his hair and her tongue sought his. Everything inside of him came to life.

So she wasn't going to hold a grudge against him for that morning, but it wouldn't be long before Alex confided in her that he'd taken that dark dive into his past. And, if things got as serious as he'd like them to, he'd need to tell her everything. Especially since he didn't want biological children of his own. That man's bloodline ended with him, and he'd always been sure that he'd keep it that way.

CHAPTER 9

*L*ife went back to normal on Monday morning, and it was a giant disappointment, Sarah thought.

Her alarm had gone off at five, she'd thrown on her running clothes and headed out. Two miles every morning got her blood pumping and her mood situated. Only today, she was overly occupied with thinking about Bruce and their little escapade in her car.

They might have taken too much time, and she was sure Alex was more than a little curious as to why, but he hadn't asked.

As she returned home, just as the sun began to paint the horizon, her phone chimed. She looked down at it as she pulled the earphones from her ears. *Good morning, beautiful. I miss you. Have a wonderful day.*

Her heart squeezed in her chest. Oh, that didn't suck, she thought.

I miss you too she replied and then pushed open the front door.

Her mother sat at the kitchen table having her morning coffee when Sarah walked through, pulled the orange juice out of the refrigerator, and drank it right from the carton.

"I suppose it will be best for you to have your own place again," her mother said. "It makes me crazy when you do that."

Sarah laughed. "You don't like orange juice," she reminded her.

"It doesn't mean I want my daughter drinking out of the container."

Sarah put the container back. "You're up and dressed extra early today."

"I'm taking Celia Rose for the day. Her babysitter is unavailable."

"Now I'm disappointed that I don't get to stick around all day."

"She does love her auntie," her mother said before taking a sip of her coffee.

"It is my life's mission to spoil those kids rotten," she mused.

"You're inching toward thirty. Don't you think about kids?"

Sarah sucked in a breath and gave it a moment of serious thought. "I suppose I always assumed I'd have kids. But I don't live my life planning for it. I have Celia Rose and I'll have the new baby to spoil too. And, I think they have one more in them," she teased. "If I don't have kids, I'll be okay with that," she said, but then she'd never had the right man to think about having kids with.

"And if you do?"

She leaned down and kissed her mother on the cheek. "I hope I'm as good a mother as you are."

WHEN SARAH BOUNDED DOWN THE STAIRS TO GET HER TRAVEL MUG filled, she saw her brother sitting at the table feeding Celia Rose.

"Why are you doing that if she's here to spend the day with Mom?" Sarah asked as she bent to kiss her niece on the top of her head.

"She took a phone call."

"From who?"

"I don't know," he snipped the words out and Sarah winced.

"In a foul mood this morning?"

"Mom said you were thinking of having Bruce move in with you to save you both some money."

The sentence socked her in the gut, but she turned toward the coffee maker so that he didn't see the expression on her face. "It was a thought. It would get him out of your basement and Mom would feel better if I wasn't alone."

"It's a little too cozy for my taste," he said, and that had her turning around.

"I don't think you get a say."

"I think I do," he argued. "You're my sister. He's my best friend."

"And wouldn't it be nice if we were in the same place helping each other out?"

He wiped off Celia Rose's face. "Do you know how he feels about you?" he asked in a hushed tone.

"I'd like to think he likes me because I'm a decent person," she said in an equally soft tone.

"You don't need the complications of him in your life that intimately."

"You don't get to tell me that."

"I'm protecting you."

"From what?"

Alex puckered his lips. "I don't know. He's a great guy and he could use a break," he said as his shoulders dropped and he took his daughter from the high chair and held her to him. "Let's just say he doesn't think of you as a little sister."

"I'm not his little sister."

"You know what the hell I mean. I don't want him getting any ideas in his head that he should consider your invitation as an offer."

"An offer to what?" she asked, but threw in that teasing voice to make him continue.

"God, don't make me say these things around my daughter."

"Oh, but I want to hear it."

Alex actually covered Celia Rose's ears. "I don't want him to think he can just have sex with you."

"He's a sexy man."

"I mean it, Sarah. You'd be one of a string of women. He doesn't do long term. He's not the kind of guy who would get married and have kids. You don't deserve that."

"Why do you think I want that from him?"

"I didn't say you wanted it. I think he has unrealistic thoughts about you, that's all."

Oh, she knew the kinds of thoughts. The man brought all the thoughts to the bedroom, and she'd admit, they'd both been around the block, so maybe they knew a thing or two and that had spiced things up. She wasn't going to get worked up over the number.

"I'm a big girl, Alex. I don't need you to protect me anymore. Besides, it's just a nice gesture. And, for your information, he's interested in rooming with me. As long as you don't need the rent money."

He shook his head. "We'd be okay without it."

"Good."

"Is that what took you so long last night on your trip to the grocery store?" he finally asked.

Sarah turned back to the refrigerator and pulled the coffee creamer out, then added it to her mug. Oh, if he knew what they'd been doing in the parking lot of the grocery store, he'd kill them both. But just thinking about it made her giddy.

"Yeah," she finally said. "We had a nice long talk about it."

CHAPTER 10

The weather was holding out, and instead of winter hanging around in late March, it was pretending to be spring in Colorado. Sarah sat at her desk, tapping her pen to her chin. She had another hour of work and she could leave.

What kind of day did Bruce put in, she wondered? Until Toby put the gym into the headquarters' office, she'd usually pass by Bruce as she left the YMCA and he walked in. Maybe, if he could get away too, they could go for a hike before it got too dark and too cold.

Emily poked her head around the cubicle wall and smiled in Sarah's direction. "How was the wedding?" she asked, and Sarah had to think about what wedding she was talking about.

"Oh, this weekend?"

"Yeah, the couple that got remarried."

Sarah smiled. "It was really nice. It was a small wedding and a big reception."

"Lots of hot prospectives?"

"I suppose," Sarah said easing back in her seat.

"And which one did you hook up with?"

If the question had come from anyone else, Sarah would have

ended the conversation right there. But she and Emily were as tight as Alex and Bruce—and the rest of the gang.

"I didn't say I did," she lifted her brows.

"And, you didn't say you didn't." Emily rolled her chair so that she was fully in Sarah's cubicle. "Who?"

"I'm not going to tell you."

"I envy you. I mean I like being married and all. But those first time kisses and stuff, man, I miss that."

"Maybe you shouldn't have married the first man that told you he loved you," Sarah jabbed.

"It just worked out that way. Besides, you might get all the hotties and have mind blowing first time sex, but married sex," she let out a hum, "it's amazing."

"Amazing?"

"Sure. It's whenever you want it. It's safe to explore. It's amazing." She smiled. "But, yeah, that first time stuff…" she whistled.

And hadn't it been just that? Their first time?

Even when she thought about their first real kiss on New Year's Eve, it still stirred her up. But the minute he put his hands on her bare skin…

"You just swooned," Emily said. "Who was it? I'm not leaving without a name."

"You're going to have to."

"Because you didn't get his name?" Emily swatted at her. "Oh my God!"

"Would you be quiet." Sarah looked around the office. "I know his name."

"You've met him before?"

"Yes."

Emily narrowed her eyes. "Do I know him?"

"Yes," Sarah said and then wished she'd lied.

The phone on Emily's desk rang. "Crap. I'm going to figure this out," she promised as she rolled her chair back to her desk, and Sarah wondered if she would be honest when Emily did figure it out.

∽

IT HAD BECOME ROUTINE TO MEET TOBY IN THE GYM AT LUNCH time. Bruce pulled up on the rower next to Toby and realized he was at least three miles behind.

"How long have you been in here?" he asked as he began to row.

"Half hour. Forty minutes. I've lost track."

"Am I late?"

Toby blew out a breath. "I had a meeting that got me worked up, so I thought I'd get started early."

"Anything you can tell me about? I'm a good ear."

Toby laughed. "Yeah, I lost a million dollars in a shady deal."

Bruce stopped rowing. "A million dollars?" he asked and looked around to see that no one was nearby. "God, what are you worth?"

"As if I would tell anyone in the world that."

"Not even me? I've wiped your puke off my shoes."

Toby stopped rowing. He took the towel he'd laid on the machine and wiped his face. "And that's why I wouldn't tell you. You and the guys, you don't see me as the name on the building or on your paycheck. To you I'm just the ugliest of you all, the lamest, and the loneliest."

"Think a lot of yourself, huh?"

Toby reached for his bottle of water and took a sip while Bruce kept rowing. "I'm just the odd man out. You all were friends. I mean you and Alex grew up together. Ray and Craig grew up together. I transplanted here."

"I'd like to think that we don't really make you feel that way."

"You don't." Toby laughed again. "But until Coach died, and we all started hanging out together again, it was pretty lonely."

"You're right."

"And if I know anything, it's that money can't buy you love," Toby picked up the handle and began rowing again. "Of course, I guess I'm the last of us to settle in, huh? You're not so lonely anymore."

Bruce's hands slipped from the handle and it zipped back against the machine with a loud thud. "I what?"

Toby stopped rowing again and laughed. "Am I the only one that knows?"

"Knows what?"

"What you did at the wedding reception?"

Bruce's mouth had gone dry. "What exactly did I do?"

"It was more like who you did."

Bruce's vision blurred. "What did you see?"

Toby leaned in toward him. "I love you like a brother and her like a sister. It will never leave my lips, I promise."

"Tell me what you saw."

The grin on Toby's face grew wider. "Sarah Burke, huh? Alex is going to kill you."

CHAPTER 11

Are you free for dinner?

Sarah smiled at the message on her phone. How was it that even though she'd had eyes for Bruce for years, suddenly just knowing he was thinking of her made her head delightfully swim?

She typed in her reply. *YES!*

Meet me at the top of Lookout Mountain.

Sarah read the message and reread it. What on earth was he planning?

Before she'd left work, Bruce had sent another text telling her the time and she should wear good shoes and a jacket. Did they seriously think enough alike that he was proposing a hike?

The thought that if he moved in with her, they wouldn't have to sneak around. But, for the next few weeks, it would be thrilling all the same. And how creative could they get?

Although, they would have to come up with some hotel money or something, because they both were much too tall to be having sex in her car. The thought humored her, and she must have laughed loud enough that Emily slid her chair around again.

"What's going on?" she asked.

"Just had a funny thought. I'm going to head out. I'm done here," Sarah said as she grabbed her bag from under her desk.

"I've seen that grin of yours before. Get your work done and be out of here by three? You're going to go meet someone."

"You don't get that from my smile. You're a big fat liar."

"I'm just really wanting you to drop that name."

"Like I said, it ain't going to happen." Sarah laughed as she stood and kissed her friend on the top of the head. "But maybe I'll go have some still new-to-me sex."

"Oh yeah," Emily called after her. "Well tonight my name is Jane and his is Tarzan."

Sarah laughed as she walked out of the office. If there was a soul she would tell, it would be Emily. But for now, Bruce Griffin was her little secret.

BRUCE SAT IN THE BACK OF HIS SUV, THE HATCH UP, AND HE waited for her. His pack sat next to him. As the sun got lower in the sky, the March air turned crisp. There weren't near as many hikers as there would be during the day, and the thought of pushing Sarah's back up against a tree while he kissed her senseless was warming his body enough he had to unzip his jacket.

He stood as he saw her car round the last corner. She parked next to him, turned off the engine, and flew from her car and right into his arms.

Her mouth came to his hot and heavy as if she'd waited all day to be together, too.

Her tongue slipped through his lips, his hands gripped her hips, and she pressed against him.

"I've waited all day for that," she said as she pressed her forehead to his.

"Yeah," he sucked in a breath. "So have I."

She stepped back. "Are we going on a hike?"

"I thought it would be a nice end to the day. We can make it short enough that we can watch the sunset from here."

She nodded, but it was the smile on her lips that entranced him. "I almost called you to see if you wanted to go for a hike," she said. "Is it weird that we think alike?"

"Not really," he offered as he pulled his pack from the car. "We've been around each other most of our lives. We run into each other all the time, and spend our free time together. I think it all makes sense."

"Yeah, but we never did this before." She moved to him again and kissed him hard enough he staggered back against the car.

"Oh, but I thought about it," he admitted when she pulled away.

Bruce locked his car and they headed toward the trail. The breeze began to nip at his cheeks.

Two steps in front of him, Sarah pulled her hair up with her hands and secured it with a band she'd had around her wrist. He took a moment to admire the view in front of him.

She was five-foot-nine, and had always hated it. But when she was around him and the guys, who all cleared at least six-foot-two, she could be herself. Sarah had more basketball skills than the fabulous five all together. The full ride scholarships and awards proved it.

At twenty-six, she'd seen the world, which was something that Bruce envied. Since he'd been planted in Colorado, he'd only left a few times, and he was damn sure to stay west of the Mississippi.

"You're lagging behind, Griffin," she called out and he laughed.

"I'm not either. Your ass is better than any of this majestic scenery," he returned and heard her laugh.

"Well then, enjoy."

Oh, he would, he thought as he jogged up to her and grabbed her from behind.

She let out a gasp, that might have sounded like a scream to anyone who around—but there was no one around.

Pulling her from the trail, he kept hold of her until they were in an area that was wooded enough no one could see them. And just as he'd imagined, he spun her around and pushed her back up against the tree, only her head hit first.

"Shit!" she let out the curse as she rubbed her head. "A little forceful, huh?"

Bruce choked on a breath and he stepped back. "I'm sorry. Oh, God, I'm sorry. I thought this would be fun. Shit. Shit!"

"Hey, I'm okay," she said as she lowered her hand. "Don't freak out. You didn't really hurt me."

"Let's go. We can go to dinner or something else. Let's get out of here."

BRUCE STARTED BACK UP THE TRAIL, BUT SARAH REACHED FOR HIM. "Hold up," she said as she turned him toward her. His eyes had gone dark, and they were shrouded with worry. "What's going on?"

"Nothing. We just need to go."

"I thought we were going to spend time together. I thought maybe," she smiled, "we were going to have some fun in the brush."

"I think we need to get out of here." He turned and walked back toward the path and kept walking.

Sarah turned around and looked out toward the trees. What had happened? She wasn't hurt. Was there something in the trees he'd seen?

When they reached the cars, Bruce paced before he opened his hatch and threw his bag inside.

Sarah slowed as she approached him. "How about some dinner?"

Bruce stopped pacing, scrubbed his hands over his face, and finally turned to look at her.

His cheeks were streaked red, as if he'd cried walking back to the cars.

"Bruce, what's going on? What's wrong with you?"

He took a breath, and then another before he moved to her. "I love you."

"I love you, too. I think we've established this part."

"I'm going to tell you what's wrong."

"Okay, go ahead."

"When we got down there, I started thinking about my dad."

And this opened a new can of worms, she thought. "What about him."

"Nothing. Just he crossed my mind and he's been doing that a lot lately."

"Do you ever see him?"

"Not since I was ten," he admitted. "And I don't ever plan to. But once in a while he gets in my head, and this is what happens. I've been seeing someone for it my whole life. But if you want to run…"

"I'm not going anywhere."

"You might change your mind."

She slid up to him and slipped her arms around him. "I've known you for twenty years. I don't know anything about your dad, but I know all about you. There's a reason I feel safe with you. There's a reason I let you touch me. There's a reason I love you."

He lifted his hands to her cheeks. "I want to spend the night with you."

Now she laughed. "I have no idea how we're going to manage that."

"What time does your mom go to bed?"

"Nine."

"I'll be there at ten." He smiled at her. "What time does she get up?"

Sarah shrugged. "I go out to run at five. Sometime after that."

"Then I'll walk out the door with you at five."

"This is where it gets exciting, huh?" She leaned in and kissed him. "You'll move in with me in six weeks?"

"I think it's the only thing that will keep us sane."

CHAPTER 12

*H*er mother's door closed and locked at nine-thirty. Sarah let out a breath and texted Bruce.

She just went to bed.

Because her hands shook, Sarah walked to the kitchen to finish loading the dishwasher. In all her life, she'd never snuck someone into the house. No, she knew the quietest way out, but sneaking someone in, that was new.

I just told your brother I was headed out for the night. He gave me a high-five. I'll be to you in twenty.

Sarah's heart hammered in her chest. God, she was twenty-six-years-old and hiding. She was sneaking men into her mother's house, and the man was lying to her brother. Okay, it wasn't a lie. Alex just didn't have all the details.

She laughed as she wiped down the counters. Okay, so this relationship was keeping the excitement in her life. But it wouldn't be like this for long. He'd said he'd move in with her.

From an observer's standpoint, she could see where someone might think they were taking it way too fast. They'd been together all of three days. But from where she sat, it had been years in the making.

Bruce Griffin had felt the same way about her as she had about him. Who would have thought? And even better, it wasn't just like—it was love.

She thought of how giddy she'd get when he'd tease her brother about making moves on her. Oh, Alex could get worked up quickly over that. They'd kissed in front of him, on the mouth, but nothing like they did now. How many dances had they had over the years, and she wrote them off as opportunity for her and just kindness on Bruce's part?

Sarah tightened her ponytail and felt the bump on the back of her head from where she'd hit the tree. Why had that set Bruce off like that? Their new relationship was completely reckless, and that impromptu move up against the tree fit right into it. What had crossed his mind when she'd hit her head?

Sarah gave it some thought. He'd mentioned that he'd thought about his dad.

Leaning against the counter, she rubbed the bump. What was it about that moment that made him think of his dad? What had his dad done to go to jail?

There were a lot of questions, and she supposed whatever he'd done, reflected in who Bruce was.

Though she'd never seen reason to check him out, maybe tomorrow she would search for information on him. She would have done it on any man she'd met and slept with.

That swirled in her gut for a moment. Perhaps she should be a little more selective with the men she'd taken to bed and not dated.

No, she wasn't going to apologize to herself for being the woman that she was. If men could do it, so could women. It didn't mean she was a slut, or easy. It meant she was secure in who she was and she enjoyed a little adventure.

And this thing with Bruce was absolutely the biggest adventure of her life. It was worth settling down if she could have Bruce.

I'm here, her phone displayed the message and her heart began to race with the anticipation of seeing him, holding him, keeping him close all night long.

Go to the back door, she replied as she walked toward it and pulled it open.

A moment later she saw him walk around the house and up the back steps. Without a word, she gathered him in her arms and dove into a kiss that had sparks of light forming behind her eyelids.

It didn't matter what his father had done, or what her brother was going to think of the situation, she thought as he lifted her up and she wrapped her legs around his waist. She loved the man, and that was all that mattered.

IT WAS JUST PAST FOUR-THIRTY IN THE MORNING AND SARAH WOKE to Bruce rubbing small circles on her shoulder with his thumb.

"We have a half hour to sleep. Why are you awake?" she whispered.

"Celia Rose wakes up at this time every day. I just realized it."

"She's not here," she reminded him.

"Yeah, but I guess I'm programmed."

Sarah turned in his arms. "I'm so glad you stayed last night."

"So am I. Though what does it say about us? We both live in the basement of one of your relatives' houses."

She buried her face in his chest. "Yeah, but not for long."

"Alex isn't going to like it."

Sarah rose up on her elbow. "I don't give a shit. The only reason I'm fine with not saying anything to him is because you don't need to put up with him until then. He'll give you a hard time, and there is no reason for him to care that you're with me."

"Oh, I think he has valid reasons."

"Then what is it?"

Bruce soothed his hand over her shoulder again and laid her back, rolling atop of her. "Your brother knows every single thing about me. Maybe he thinks I'm not good for you."

"If he knows every single thing about you, then he knows you're a good man and I'd be lucky to have you with me the rest of my life."

"I like your version."

"Bruce, if there's something else…"

"There is nothing else," he said as he pressed his lips to hers. "All you need to know is that I love you, and I've always loved you."

She looked up at him in the shadows of the room. "We've wasted so much time."

"We'll make up for it."

CHAPTER 13

*A*s Sarah climbed from her car on Sunday morning, she noticed her brother and his family walk through the front door of the YMCA.

It would be the first time she'd get to see Bruce since she woke up in his arms on Monday. The dating in secret thing came with its share of obstacles.

"I've missed you," his voice came from behind her and she turned to see him walking toward her.

He moved in, wrapped his arms around her waist, and kissed her exactly how she'd expect him to when they hadn't seen each other in a week.

"Someone is going to see us," she said as he eased back.

"For the record, Toby knows."

She sucked in a breath and he held up a finger to ward off anything she was contemplating.

"He's known since the wedding. He saw us," Bruce continued. "He's not going to say anything."

"Well, I suppose we just have to be prepared for the wrath and take it. I mean, we're just prolonging the inevitable."

"We could walk into that gym hand in hand, just like

Catherine and Alex did when they so subtly announced that they were together."

Sarah laughed. "That took me by surprise." She blew out a breath. "I didn't care that he had fallen in love with Catherine. I still thought she hated him. I'm not ready for that. I'm not ready to out us like Catherine and Alex did."

She searched his eyes. "I don't get the feeling Alex is joking when he says I'm forbidden to you."

Bruce nodded. "I think you're right." He hiked his bag up on his shoulder. "It's going to hurt him no matter how we tell him. But Sunday morning at basketball isn't the way to handle it."

"C'mon, let's go in there and kick their asses."

"It's the highlight of my week—well it was until I got drunk at a wedding and took home this amazing woman."

Sarah laughed. This was more like it. The banter they shared was what drove her from week to week.

"God, I hope she was worth it," Sarah said as she closed her car door and pulled her bag up on her shoulder.

"She makes me sneak around, but it keeps me young. I feel like I'm seventeen again."

She lifted a brow. "Rumor has it you're much more skilled than that."

"I like the rumor. Go on."

She shook her head as they neared the entrance. "We'll discuss that in depth later."

BRUCE WAS LAUGHING WHEN HE FOLLOWED HER INTO THE GYM, and immediately he noticed Alex's gaze fall on them. It was his usual glare when he'd see them together, so how come this time it felt raw?

Bruce decided it wasn't that Alex was seeing it different, he was. Before, if he spent time with Sarah, and Alex would comment, it was all in fun. It was innocent and aimed to piss Alex off. Now the feelings that were being shared between him and Sarah were real, and there was something going on—and man, was it going on.

Acting as if it were any other Sunday, Bruce dropped his bag next to Alex's and sat down on the bench next to him. He made eyes at Celia Rose, who smiled back at him.

"She's getting so big," Bruce said. "In no time there'll be a gate at the top of the stairs for me to climb over."

Catherine bounced Celia Rose on her knee. "It arrived yesterday. Be prepared."

Bruce laughed. "Noted."

Alex pulled on his shoes and tied them, but he didn't look in Bruce's direction. When he stood up and walked out onto the court without a word, Bruce looked in Catherine's direction.

"What's wrong with him?" he asked.

Catherine looked at her daughter and kissed the top of her head. "His mom said something to him about you moving out and in with Sarah."

"Really?" He tied his shoe. "Sarah mentioned it. She said she thought her mom would feel better about her having a roommate."

Catherine nodded. "Their mom is fine with it. Alex seems to have a problem with it."

"Yeah, well he's had this same stick up his ass for twenty years. I'm sure it's petrified by now." He tied the other shoe.

Catherine slid next to him and put her hand on his arm. "Don't be angry with him. He's always going to protect her."

"Against me," he whispered. "It's hard not to take it personally."

Bruce stood up and headed out on the court. Today he teamed with Ray and Craig against Alex, Toby, and Sarah. Odds were stacked against them. Sarah's team always won, and Alex seemed to have a vendetta against him personally.

Within the first ten minutes of the game, he'd taken a

shoulder and an elbow to the chest. At one point when Rachel's baby let out a cry, and he turned to look, Alex's pass missed and hit him in the side of the head.

"I'm beginning to think this game has become personal," Bruce said as he stood on the sideline to throw the ball in.

"Maybe it has," Alex replied through gritted teeth. "Throw in the damn ball."

With his eyes locked on Alex's, he noticed Ray out of the corner of his eye and threw the ball. The action was on the court, but Alex and Bruce stayed right where they were, staring at each other.

When Craig celebrated his dunk, the play stopped and they all moved back toward Alex and Bruce.

Toby rested a hand on Alex's shoulder. "Hey, what's going on?"

Nothing was said.

Sarah moved in between them and faced her brother. "What's wrong with you?"

Alex's eyes moved to his sister. "I want to hear what he has to say about your new living arrangement."

"My living arrangement? I live with Mom."

His lips pursed. "About when you get your new place."

Sarah's hands came to her waist. "Like I told you the other morning, that is none of your damn business."

"It is when you're moving in with him," he said as he nodded in Bruce's direction.

"And what is wrong with me?" Bruce moved in next to Sarah.

"I have always told you, she's off limits."

As Bruce took a breath to counter that, Sarah shoved her hands against her brother's chest. "You don't get to say shit about it. It's my house. He needs a place to live other than your basement. Mom would like me to have a roommate. You're being a goddamned asshole!"

Now Rachel was on her feet, infant in her arms.

"Guys, you need to settle this somewhere else," she said calmly. "They're about to send security in here."

"I don't have to settle this with anyone," Sarah said as she took another step closer to Alex. "Stay the hell out of my business."

"It is my business."

"You're not Dad. I can live with anyone I want. And I can't think of a better person than Bruce to share my new home with. So you can accept it and be part of it. Or you can choose to not be part of it. But it is none of your damn business."

And with that, they all watched Sarah turn away, pick up her bag, and walk out of the gym.

Alex turned his attention back to Bruce, but before he could say another word, Catherine moved between them.

"You guys can have this discussion privately at home."

CHAPTER 14

*A*lex followed Sarah's example. He picked up his bag, and the diaper bag, and headed toward the door with Catherine scrambling to follow with Celia Rose.

Bruce took a moment to sit down and change out his shoes. It was hard not to take it all personally when Alex acted like that.

Rachel sat down next to him. "He'll calm down."

"He can shove his calm right up his ass," Bruce said as he pulled off his high tops and dropped them into his bag. "I get wanting to protect his family. But it's me. He should be happy for us. He should be okay with me being part of her life."

"Happy for you to move in together? Or is there something else?" she whispered.

"It wouldn't matter either way. I'm obviously not good enough for his family."

Rachel rested her hand on his arm. "Don't think that way. He'll come around."

"At this moment, I just don't care."

Bruce slid on his street shoes, gathered his bag, and stood. Then, after taking a breath, he bent and kissed Rachel on the cheek and Angela on the top of the head. "I'll be okay," he assured her, then walked out of the gym without saying a word to anyone else.

As he threw his bag into the back of his car, he watched Toby run through the parking lot toward him. He supposed it was to be expected, they all would eventually take their shot with him.

"Hold up," Toby called out as Bruce opened his door. "What's going on with you two?"

"Don't worry about it."

"Does he know you're seeing Sarah?"

"Not unless you told him I was," he bit out the words and watched Toby's reaction carefully.

"I didn't say a word," he admitted, and there was no reason for Bruce to think otherwise.

"I didn't suppose you did. I think this is all about us moving in together. I guess it'll come as a shock when he finds out how much I love her."

A smile formed on Toby's lips. "You deserve it. And, wow, with Sarah. I thought you two were always just flirting to make him mad."

"It was a bonus. Now I'm really afraid his head will explode."

Toby leaned against the car. "Listen, I know what an ass he can be. And I know this is going to put a strain on your living arrangement. So, I was thinking, if you're interested, you could live in the guest house until Sarah's place is done."

"Really?"

"Yeah. It'll help me out too. I have some traveling to do, and you could keep an eye on things. I'll only be gone a few weeks, but I'd rather have someone out there."

"You have no idea what this means to me."

"I think I do," he stood and held his hand out. "What do you say?"

Bruce shook his hand, and then pulled him in for a hug. "I say I owe you."

"And I won't say a word if Sarah stays with you."

~

Can you meet me? Let's talk. She looked at the text while she was stopped at the light.

Sarah wasn't sure she wanted to talk to anyone. Though she was headed home, and in the mood she was in, even her mother was going to get an earful.

In fact, she thought again, maybe she should head to her brother's and just let him have it. What would he say when he found out not only was she moving in with Bruce, but she'd been sleeping with him too—in Alex's own house!

When the light turned green, she threw down her phone, gripped the steering wheel, and pulled over into a parking lot.

Picking up her phone, she returned the text. *Where?*

She didn't know what else to say.

Where are you now? Bruce replied.

Sarah looked up to see where she'd parked. *Walmart parking lot.*

She waited for his reply.

I'll be there in ten.

Sarah rested her head back against the seat. This wasn't supposed to be complicated—her falling in love. It should have been the best time of her life, so why did it have to come with all this angst?

Would Alex be like this if it were anyone else? Was he that protective of her? And why couldn't he just be happy for her? Bruce was his best friend. It was ridiculous for him to be mad. Wasn't it supposed to be the perfect fairy tale to have your sibling fall in love with your best friend?

The tears stung her eyes, but she refused to let them fall.

She wanted the happily ever after, and she wanted it with Bruce—but she didn't want to lose her family over it.

. . .

Just as Bruce had said, he pulled into the lot ten minutes later and parked next to Sarah.

As he climbed from his car, she did the same. Her eyes were red from tears, and he couldn't help but pull her into his arms and hold her.

"He's going to have to get over this," he said as he pressed kisses to her hair.

"He's an asshole."

"No one knows that better than me."

"I love you. You're what's important," she said as she sucked in a breath. "I only want to be with you."

Her words made his heart swell. How did he get so lucky?

"Listen," he eased her back and wiped the tears from her cheeks. "I got an offer, and I think you're going to like it."

"An offer?"

"Yeah. Toby has a guest house behind that monstrosity he lives in. He's offered it to me to live in, and he says you can come with me. We can stay until your place is ready."

Her eyes widened. "We could be together?"

"We could. And we wouldn't be sneaking into anyone's house."

That caused her to laugh. "Don't take it personally, but when I see Toby again, I'm going to kiss him so hard, right on the mouth."

"I'll make sure to look the other direction."

"When can we move in?"

"I suppose as soon as we show up with stuff. It's a fully furnished guest house. All you need to do is pack some clothes."

CHAPTER 15

Because he wasn't in the mood for confrontation, Bruce decided to head over to Toby's instead of going home. Perhaps he could borrow some clothes, and then when he knew Alex was at work on Monday, he'd go and pack.

It wouldn't take him but a minute to be out of Alex's house.

Besides, it was time. It was one thing to have moved in when it was Craig's house, and Craig was single. Then Craig sold it to Alex, and then Alex got married too.

It was time for Bruce to be out.

Of course, now he was underfoot for Toby, but things were different there. This was an extra house, and he wouldn't have to skirt around Toby at all.

When he pulled into Toby's driveway, he was surprised to find him in the driveway hand washing his BMW.

Bruce laughed as he stepped out of his car. "You don't have someone to do that for you?"

"Why? This is enjoyable."

"You're a mystery, friend. You have this enormous house to yourself and you do everything on your own."

Toby shrugged. "This is my only extravagance. Who knows, maybe someday I'll fill it with kids."

"You'd better get on that."

Toby laughed. "Right?" He turned off the water. "Did you come to look at the house?"

"Actually, I came to just live in it. I thought I'd give Alex some time to cool down. So, if you don't mind, can I borrow some clothes for work tomorrow?"

Toby nodded with a smile. "Of course." He set the hose on the ground and picked up the sponge. "Do you think you and Alex are going to get through this?"

"Oh, it'll get worse before it gets better. I mean, I'm not only moving in with his sister. I'd like to think things would progress to where we could talk about getting married."

"Damn. I didn't realize it's been going on that long."

"The actual her and I hasn't, but really, this has been building for twenty years. It's about time."

"Bruce Griffin, husband and father."

"Oh, no. I'll never be a father," he said in defense.

"Why?"

"I don't want kids."

"Really?"

"Yeah, why is that such a surprise?" he asked.

"I don't know. I just thought that's what everyone wanted, who finds someone to marry."

"Well not me."

Toby dropped the sponge and picked the hose back up. "What does Sarah think about that?"

Bruce shrugged. "We haven't talked about it. I guess I should say, I wouldn't mind having kids, but I don't want biological ones."

"I don't understand."

"Let's just say my dad had some undesirable genetics that I don't want to pass on."

Toby nodded slowly. "I never thought about things like that. What did he have?"

Bruce gave it some thought. "He had some mental disorders. It's just better to let that die off with him."

Toby let out a hum of acceptance, and continued to finish cleaning his car.

~

THE INSTRUCTIONS TO GET TO THE GUEST HOUSE WERE programmed into Sarah's phone. As she passed the main house, she smiled.

Oh, to think that her and Bruce had started there on New Year's Eve with that kiss that Ray broke up before Alex caught them.

As she drove the dirt road up the hill, past the house, the tennis court, and the pool, she saw the small guest house come into view.

If she had to guess, the guest house was the original house on the property. A small log cottage with a wrap-around porch greeted her.

The sky was orange with the setting sun, and the lights from inside the cottage gave the house a warmth that drew her in.

Sarah parked her car next to Bruce's and pulled her bag from the back seat as he walked out onto the porch in his jeans, a T-shirt, and his bare feet.

Wasn't that a sight? She was coming home to him, and her heart did a little tumble when she saw him standing there.

"I didn't even know this was back here," she said as she closed the car door and walked toward the house.

"It's cute. We may never want to leave."

Sarah laughed as she walked up the front steps. "As long as we get to be together, I don't care where we are." She leaned into him and kissed him.

As she pulled back she studied him. Worry still clouded his eyes.

"Are you okay? I mean, today sucked," she said.

Bruce ran his hand down her arm. "I'm fine. Alex and I will be fine. The important thing is that you're here, and we can just be us."

"I like that."

Bruce took her bag from her hand. "I made dinner," he said as he opened the front door and she stepped into the aroma.

"Roast?"

"It was my grandfather's favorite. My grandmother taught me how to make it when I moved in with them. It's always been my welcome home meal."

Sarah gazed up at him. "I think that's very sweet. Your grandfather was always such a nice man. And your grandmother always spoiled me with cookies."

"Baking makes her happy. She doesn't do as much of it as she used to. She can't see as well. But she still tries her hand at it."

"What will she think of us?" Sarah asked as she took Bruce's free hand and held it in hers.

"She won't be surprised at all. If anyone has always known my secret, it's been her." Bruce set her bag down on the coffee table and pulled her in close. "I love you."

Sarah let out a sigh. "And I love you."

"Will you be okay still loving me, even if Alex doesn't come around?"

She rested her head to his chest, and wrapped her arms around him tighter. "He'll come around."

"That wasn't my question."

Sarah eased back. "I love you. It's his loss if he doesn't accept this. But we weren't raised to go silent between us. I can't lose my niece and the baby that's on the way. He knows that. So, he might hold a grudge, but..."

Bruce kissed her forehead. "I get it. I'll do everything I can on my side to make things easier. I don't want to lose him either."

"My mom is fine with it. You need to know that."

He smiled. "That helps. And for the record, your family always made me feel welcome. I've been surrounded by that love, and scolded by it too. It makes for some happy memories."

"And it makes Alex that much more an asshole." She brushed her fingers through his hair. "I don't know why he's like this."

"I think I might, but we'll talk about that later. Right now, we're going to go in the kitchen and eat dinner. Then we'll clean up, like a normal couple, and maybe then enjoy a beer on the front porch as we listen to the sounds of the trees in the breeze."

"That sounds like the perfect night."

oby had given Bruce the morning off to go and get his things from Alex's house. He'd offered an armed escort too, but Bruce assumed that was a joke.

The house was quiet when he walked through the back door. Catherine's car hadn't been in the driveway, and neither had Alex's. Perhaps he could manage to get in and out before either of them came home.

He hated feeling as if he were sneaking around. Damnit, this shouldn't be a problem.

Bruce pulled his suitcase from the closet and began to fill it with clothes from his dresser. Most of his personal belongings were in storage in his grandmother's garage, but the truth of the matter was, he didn't own much.

It seemed as if he never wanted to be bogged down with items. After all, he'd once been pulled from his bed in the middle of the night and forced to change lives. Everything he'd held dear to him had been taken away. Maybe he just didn't want that kind of pain again.

He was sure that crossed his mind because of the call he'd had with his therapist on the drive to Alex's. For the past few years,

Bruce had been able to talk about the mundane. Work, friends, his grandfather's death, and his grandmother's ailing health. But now they were working through the fact that his father was on his mind. That there was some biographical bullshit going to air on TV where they were going over his father's case. And of course, they dove into his relationship with Sarah and Alex, and the strain it was causing.

In the end he wouldn't let it break up Sarah's family, even if he had to step away, but he didn't want to have to do that. He wanted to work it out with Alex.

Before he could zip up the suitcase and finish boxing up the few personal items he had sprinkled around the apartment, he heard the back door.

"Bruce, are you down there?" Catherine called.

"I am."

He heard the footsteps and saw her reach the bottom of the stairs as he walked out of the bathroom with a few toiletries.

"Are you going somewhere?" she asked.

"Toby is letting me stay in his guest house. I think it's best for right now. You and Alex don't need me here."

Catherine hiked Celia Rose up on her hip, and adjusted her around her small mound of a belly. "I hate this. What's really going on?"

"Listen, Alex has his reasons for not wanting me around Sarah. I get it. But you guys need to be a family without worrying who I brought home, or what I can hear."

Her eyes went wide. "How much do you hear?"

Bruce chuckled. "Enough. It's just time for me to go."

He dropped the toiletries in the suitcase as Catherine moved toward him. Resting her hand on his arm, she studied him. "What's going on with you and Sarah? It's more than just a roommate agreement, isn't it?"

Bruce chewed his bottom lip. "I don't want to say anything."

"Okay, then let me tell you what I know. I know that on New Year's Eve, there was talk that you two were making out."

"There was, huh?"

"Yes. And I saw her sneak away during the wedding reception. Now when I asked her about it, she said she might have gone to the bathroom, but…"

"That's what she said?"

"Yes."

"And who told you we were making out?"

Catherine's shoulders dropped. "C'mon, there were a hundred people there."

Bruce ran his fingers over his brow. "I guess it was a good thing we were too drunk to remember. Okay, we did make out on New Year's. Is that why he's all up in arms?"

"I don't know if he knows. But if I know…"

"Then it's safe to assume he does too." Bruce took Catherine's hand and led her to the couch. Then he took Celia Rose from her and sat down. Catherine sat down next to them.

The little girl, who had Alex's dark eyes, smiled at him and reached for his face with her slobbery fingers. He'd miss seeing her grow up right in front of his eyes.

It wasn't forever, he promised himself. They'd work through this.

"I don't want to say too much to you," he said as Celia Rose let out a happy scream. "I wouldn't ask you to keep things from your husband. So I'll tell you that Sarah invited me to live with her in her new house. Yes, she thinks I would be better off not living in my friends' basement. And, yes, her mother is worried about her, though why is beyond me. Sarah isn't the kind of woman that would let anyone take advantage of her, or hurt her. But if her mother's happier that she has a roommate, then I'm happy to be that roommate."

"But what about the part where you're in love with her?"

Celia Rose grabbed the front of his shirt as he shifted a glance to Catherine. "I'd be surprised if that was a secret at all. I've been in love with Sarah Burke most of my life."

"And you never made a move on her because of Alex?"

"Yeah."

Catherine took her daughter's hand as she bounced up and down on Bruce's lap. "I think that's silly."

"He has his reasons. Though, I never knew what they were, except protection of his little sister. But, I think I know why now."

"Why is that?"

Bruce shook his head. "If you don't know, then there is still hope for me and Alex. It means I can still trust him."

Her brows drew together. "You have a secret he's keeping?"

"Don't we all?"

"I suppose. For what it's worth, I think you should make a move on Sarah. You both deserve happiness. And I've seen how she looks at you."

Bruce grinned as Celia Rose reached for her mother. "And how does she look at me?"

"As if she's been in love with you her entire life too."

"Well, wouldn't I be the luckiest man in the world?"

CHAPTER 17

*I*t hadn't taken long to fall into a routine with Sarah. The waking up, coffee in travel mugs, kisses goodbye. Then there was making dinner together, watching the sun set from the porch, and making love in their own bed with no one around.

It could be like this forever, Bruce thought as he walked to his car with his coffee in his hand. Aside from not having talked to Alex since Sunday, Bruce couldn't remember a time in his entire life when he'd been happier.

Bruce took in the sight before he climbed into his car. The steep mountain sides, and the trees which were filling in with greenery. Of course it all butted up to the beautiful blue Colorado sky. He'd always appreciated the scenery, but now that his heart was full, it was even more spectacular.

As he headed down the dirt road, he took a moment to look at Toby's house. He'd be heading out of town soon for business, and as promised, Bruce would keep an eye on the house.

Merging onto the highway, Bruce's thoughts went back to Sarah. He knew Alex's issue with him had to do with his father. At least that's what was in his heart. How could he convince his dearest friend that he wasn't his father? And how did he bring up the subject with Sarah?

A good relationship started with the truth. Bruce's entire life was based on a lie—even though that lie was created to save his life.

Bruce headed in the direction of his grandmother's house, which he did often before he headed into the office.

She had been his savior, hadn't she? Alex had been right, Bruce would never leave her.

Constance and Thomas Griffin had put their life on the line when they took him in. They knew what they were doing, but Bruce often wondered why.

Why, in the middle of the night, show up to the police station to claim a boy who had been pulled from his bed in Chicago and deposited in Golden, Colorado after his father had been arrested for his mother's murder—which he witnessed.

Why give that boy a good family name and adopt him after his father was found guilty of murdering eight other women?

Why continue to love him after he was an adult and their obligation was over?

Because the Griffins were the most decent people in the world, he thought as he drove down his grandmother's street. They had done right by Bruce, and working on himself, for the rest of his life, would be how he honored them.

They had to know that at any moment he could snap and slash their throats in the middle of the night. But somehow, their optimism kept Bruce in line, and his father's genetics away.

Bruce had long ago taken care of the issue that would possibly breed more men like his father. Unless a missing sibling showed up, and he supposed that was entirely possible, that blood line had stopped with him. And, soon, he'd have to discuss that with Sarah too.

When he pulled into the driveway, and stepped out of the car, he heard the screen door open and saw his grandmother standing there. She was in her nineties now, but she had the face of a woman in her seventies, she would tell him.

"Look who the cat dragged in. Just in time, I made cinnamon rolls," she said, her voice shaky with that age that her face did not give away.

"I must have known," he teased as he walked up the step and planted a noisy kiss on her cheek. "It smells so good in here," he said stepping into the house he'd been raised in.

The boy from Chicago had died the first night he'd slept in his own room and Bruce Griffin had been born.

Before he'd arrived, they'd made the room comfortable for him. Experience had taught them to even leave a journal with a lock on the desk. He'd used it—the journal and the lock. He'd asked for more over the years, and they'd always manifest.

No one ever read what he wrote. In fact, when the books were full, his grandfather would take him camping and allow him to burn them. He'd never asked one question. They would sit in silence and watch the words—the memories and the healings— go up in flames.

Walking into his grandmother's house he realized that he'd been Bruce Griffin much longer than he'd been that victim that had been pulled from the carnage of a different life.

A zip of anger shot through him. Alex Burke had nothing to worry about. Bruce wasn't his father. He was the kid raised by his grandparents on the quiet street in Golden.

"You seem to have a lot on your mind," his grandmother said as she walked past him and toward the tray of cinnamon rolls she'd set to cool. "Sit down, let's talk."

"I don't have much time. I have to get to work," he said, sitting down where she'd directed him.

"You have ten minutes. You never need more than that."

She was right. His entire life had always been put straight ten minutes at a time.

He watched his grandmother plate the cinnamon roll with the most frosting, and he smiled. That had always been his.

When she set it down on the table in front of him, she kissed the top of his head, and sat down next to him.

"Now eat," she said as she watched.

Bruce took a bite, let it melt in his mouth, and then smiled at her. "You haven't lost your touch."

"Never will. Now, what's got you so worried?"

CHAPTER 18

*N*othing ever got past his grandmother, and he supposed that's why he was there. He needed someone who knew everything and held no judgement.

"I wanted to let you know I've moved out of Alex's house."

She nodded slowly, then pulled a piece off his cinnamon roll and ate it. "Good. You are a grown man and shouldn't be living in someone's basement."

"It was necessary," he added as he took another bite of his roll. "For a few weeks, I'm living in Toby's guest house."

"There are two houses there?"

That made Bruce chuckle. "Yes. I assume this was the original house. It's tucked up closer to the mountains."

"I'd like to see that."

"I'll make sure you do," he promised. "And in a few weeks I'm moving into a new townhouse."

"New as in new to you, or new?"

"New, and new to me. But I'm moving in with a roommate."

His grandmother nodded slowly. "And you're pussyfooting around this because you're moving in with a woman."

And the reason they'd successfully raised him, was because his grandparents didn't bullshit, he thought.

"Yes."

"Lord, it's about time. You love this woman, or you're just shacking up?"

Now he smiled. "I love her."

"And you're going to let me meet her before I die?"

He didn't like that way of phrasing it at all. "You know her."

Now his grandmother's eyes narrowed on him. "No way. No way!" She slapped a hand down on his arm. "You got her?"

He couldn't help but laugh and then he moved into kiss her on the cheek. "It started on New Year's Eve with a kiss. And, well, it's just kept going."

"You have steel patience, son. And she loves you back?"

"She does," he said and it was as airy as it felt in his chest. "Maybe some communication over the years would have done us good. It appears she's always had a thing for me, but kept her spacing because of Alex. And I did the same."

His grandmother nodded slowly, and he took another bite from his roll. "And Alex is…"

"Going to blow a gasket."

"Expected," she said as she sat back in her chair, crossed her ankles, and rested her hands on her knee. "He doesn't know you're sleeping with his sister."

Now the heat rose in Bruce's cheeks. "That sounds dirty."

"It sounds like a good time. But he doesn't know?"

"No. I don't think so. But, he knows she invited me to move in with her, and we've had a few words."

"So you expect it to all go south when he finds out."

"Of course I do. For twenty years he's told me she's off limits —forbidden."

"What does she think?"

Bruce ran his finger through the frosting and licked it off. "She loves me, Gram. Like really loves me. She's willing to put it on the line for me. But, he's her family, and Alex's daughter, and the one on the way, are her life. She's made it very clear that he'll have to grow some and get over it, because she's not giving them up."

"And she knows what you did? That you won't have your own kids?"

"It's a discussion we're going to have very soon."

"And she knows who you are?"

There it was. There was the proof that he needed and why he'd gone straight to his grandmother's. He had to tell Sarah the whole truth.

"No. She knows my mom died and my dad went to jail and that's why I came here. She doesn't know they are connected, and she doesn't know who you are in relation to that."

"I'm your grandmother. That's fact."

Bruce reached for her fragile hand and held it in his. "You are. Blood doesn't mean a damned thing in my life."

"Mine either. You're going to marry her?"

"I want to."

"Then I suggest you get your stories in order and give her some space. She's going to need it to process everything. And, you'd best come clean with Alex. He deserves that."

Bruce let out a breath and collected his thoughts. "They're doing some serial killer biography series on one of those channels."

"They came looking for you?"

"No," he shook his head. "No one knows where to find me. Normality has done me well there."

"But you are afraid that if you tell them, that's two more people who know."

"Yes."

His grandmother stood from her chair and moved to him, taking his face in her hands. "You are not that man. You are my grandson. You were raised with love, care, and compassion. And do you know why it was successful?"

He shook his head, still gripped between his grandmother's tiny hands.

"Because you wanted it. You wanted normality. You wanted friends. You wanted the love we gave you. If you want Sarah, then give her space to understand what you tell her. If you want Alex, give him the same. Your circumstances differ from anything normal. Your fears are great. Your memories torturous, but you, my son, are brave and brilliant. Everything you have ever wanted will be yours. Because you believe, and you want."

She tipped his head toward her and kissed him on the forehead.

"Tell Alex I'd like to see that daughter of his, and meet his baby. I have a few years left to spoil another set of grandkids." She smiled, and he swore her eyes twinkled as if she were some fairy godmother, which, he supposed she was.

"I'll tell him."

"And I want to see Toby's big fancy house too."

He chuckled. "I'll tell him."

"And Ray, he married his wife again."

Bruce nodded. "Yes, he did. They lost their baby though."

Her eyes flashed the sadness associated with that and she sat back down in her chair. She'd lost many babies, and that's how he'd come to be her child. "You give them my best. That baby had bigger plans," she offered and he nodded again. "And what about Craig and his wife, Coach's daughter, right?"

Bruce loved that his grandmother remembered everyone who was important to him and took interest.

"Yes, they just had a daughter, Angela. She's beautiful."

"And the mom, oh, Craig's wife, what is her name?"

"Rachel."

"Right, she's doing okay after that scary situation at the school?"

He let out a sigh. He and Rachel could go rounds with shitty things that had happened to them. "Yeah, she recovered and is doing amazing. She's a therapist and she helps people."

"It sounds like you're surrounded by just the right kind of people to get you through all of this. Now finish that cinnamon roll, and take one for Toby. Then get out and go to work."

CHAPTER 19

*S*arah focused on the image on the screen. She'd taken her lunch break to look over some of the options on the townhouse as she ate lunch at her desk. There had been some consideration to call Bruce and ask him what he thought, but it was still her house. She needed to be mindful that if things didn't work out, or if Alex got in the way, it would still be her house.

When she heard movement behind her, she assumed that Emily had walked up.

"Do you like the tile for the floor, or the wood?"

"I've always liked the look of wood," her brother's voice replied.

Sarah turned to see Alex leaned up against the cubicle wall, his arms crossed in front of him and his ankles crossed leisurely.

"I didn't expect you. What are you doing here?"

"Do you have time to talk?"

Sarah looked at the clock on her desk. "I suppose I could. Let me tell Emily."

"I did. She said take all the time you need, she'll cover you."

And wasn't that convenient. "Well, let's take a walk."

. . .

Sarah walked to the stairs and down the three flights that led to the door which would take them on a path around the campus. She often walked during her lunch breaks, and she was grateful that the area had been built around the active Colorado lifestyle.

"So, what are we talking about?"

"Seriously?" Alex tucked his hands into his pockets. "Mom said that you moved out."

"I did."

"And you moved in with Bruce at Toby's. Why did you do that? Your house will be ready soon. And seriously I think if he's going to move out of my house, then Toby's was the next best thing. Maybe he should have moved in there and not with Craig in the first place. But for you to leave and move in, that's just stupid. And you don't need a roommate. You've lived on your own before and Mom is just paranoid. So what the hell are you doing?"

Because she assumed he'd run out of air, she stopped and studied him as he turned to her.

"What?" he asked.

Sarah threw her hands in the air. This was it. This was the moment.

"Listen to yourself," she said as she walked toward him. "You're a lunatic."

"I'm looking out for you."

"Why?"

"Bruce has things in his past that you don't need to be part of. And why you want to pick him up as your roommate…"

"I love him, Alex," she blurted the words out figuring it was the only way she'd get him to shut up.

Sarah was sure Alex had staggered before he moved to meet her eye to eye. "Say that again."

"I love him."

"Where in the hell did that come from?"

"You get it. You're in love."

"My wife isn't the child of..." he stopped and pursed his lips. "Catherine wasn't off limits."

"And I am?"

"Yes!"

"That was your rule, and it's absolutely stupid!"

"It's to protect you."

"From your best friend? Do you know how hypocritical that is? The man you shared your entire life with, who lived in your house, with your family, and he's not good enough for me?"

Alex gripped her shoulders. "You don't know who he is."

"Like hell I don't. Alex, I'm in love with Bruce. I have been in love with Bruce most of my life, and out of everyone, I would hope you'd know how he feels about me."

"He's not who you think he is."

"Then tell me, Alex," she said breaking free of his grip. "Who is he? Because he's been the same guy I've known my entire life. He's been the same friend who took care of you. He's been the same person I have loved for as long as I can remember."

Alex's shoulders dropped. "I didn't want this for you. You deserve better."

"I deserve the love of a man who adores me. Bruce is that man."

She could see the conflict in her brother's eyes and she knew there was more. There was something she wasn't being told, and if her brother wanted Bruce out of her life, then why wasn't he telling her what he thought he knew?

"Alex, I want you to be happy for me—for us."

"I can't. I just can't," he said as he raked his fingers through his hair. "When did all of this start?"

Sarah walked to the park bench in the shade and sat down. "New Year's Eve," she admitted as Alex sat down next to her. "We drank too much and started making out." Then she laughed. "Ray walked up on us and threw peanuts at us to get our attention because you were walking down the stairs."

"So everyone knows about this?"

She shrugged. "I don't know who knows. I don't know who suspects. Well, Toby knows."

"Obviously."

"Though, Rachel and Catherine have a pretty good feeling that they know. They saw us disappear at Ray and Kelly's wedding."

Alex closed his eyes as if something moved through him and disgusted him. "You were the woman in my basement, weren't you?"

Sarah waited until his eyes lifted and met hers again. "Yes."

"You snuck into my home to sleep with a man I forbid you to be with?" His voice had risen again.

"You're an asshole!" She stood and started back to the building, but Alex was up and following her.

When he spun her to him, she pushed him back.

"I love Bruce. Get off your high horse and be happy for me."

"You don't know who he is."

"And you're loyal enough to him that you're not spilling that on me either. So what the hell is wrong with him?"

"I'm afraid for you."

"But not for your own family?"

"I'm there to protect my family."

"You're messed up! I love Bruce. I'm going to marry Bruce, and I told him I wasn't giving up my family. And not that he asked me to do that," she confirmed. "But I want those kids in my life. I love my sister-in-law like she was my own sister, and you, you stubborn asshole, I love you. And, Alex, I love Bruce. So either you tell me what I don't know, or you let me find out. I know him, Alex. I've known him since I was five years old. He loves me."

Alex scrubbed his hands over his face. "I don't like it."

"I don't care."

"I see that." He pulled Sarah to him and wrapped his arms around her. "Be careful. That's all I can ask. But I'm not over this. I'm not giving you my blessing."

"That's really too bad," she said as she stepped back from him. "Because without Dad here, I really could use your blessing."

CHAPTER 20

*B*ruce hadn't expected Sarah to be home before him. He figured she'd stop off at the YMCA and work out before she came home. That was her routine.

Every light in the little house was on, and the windows were open. He heard the sound of music coming from inside. Or he thought it was music as he stepped out of the car.

What in the hell was she listening to? Then above the music he heard a blood curdling scream and his heart leapt into his throat.

For a moment he was paralyzed. He squeezed his eyes closed and he could hear his mother's screams coming from the other room and he could see her on the kitchen floor as his father plunged the kitchen knife in her chest over, and over, and over.

The contents of his lunch rose, and he heard her scream again.

"Get out of here! Get out!"

Sarah pushed open the front door and pushed a small mouse out of the house with a broom.

She looked up at him and he felt the blood drain from his body, and everything went dark.

. . .

SARAH WAS STANDING OVER HIM AND HE COULD HEAR THE SOUND of tires on the gravel road.

"There you are. You scared the shit out of me," she was screaming. "Don't move. You hit your head pretty hard."

"I'm okay."

"I said stay there," she was screaming again.

He thought she'd handle a little trauma better than that, but okay.

Bruce looked around. Why was he on his back in the dirt? Had he had a heart attack? Was he poisoned? Had someone attacked him?

Whoever had driven up had stopped on the gravel and jumped from their car. A moment later Toby was looking down at him too.

"I leave you in charge and you do this?" he said as he helped him sit up. "How's your head?"

"It's throbbing like a mother," Bruce replied as he put his hand to the back of his head. "No blood. I'm okay."

Sarah was crying now, and he reached for her.

"I'm okay," he repeated.

"You were just standing there. You looked at me and then you just went down."

"I'm okay." He looked up at Toby. "Help me up."

Toby hooked his hands under Bruce from behind and helped him to his feet. As soon as he stood, he reached for Sarah and then pulled her to him. "I'm okay."

"You need a doctor."

"You're right. Actually, I do."

Her eyes went wide. "Okay. I'll take you. We'll take you to the hospital."

"We'll talk about it in the house." Bruce locked eyes with her so she'd understand that he didn't want to say anything else with

Toby there. Then he turned to Toby and shook his hand. "I'm okay here."

Toby eyed him warily. "We have a doctor on staff. I can call him."

Of course he did. "I'm okay. I know what happened and I'm not hurt. I'll be okay, and I'll get checked out," Bruce promised. "You leave for your trip, and I'll take care of your house."

Toby exchanged glances between him and Sarah. "You can always reach me."

"I'm fine."

Toby nodded and headed back to his car.

"Oh, hey," Bruce called back to him. "My grandmother wants a tour of your house someday."

Again, Toby eyed him, this time cautiously before he smiled. "Will she bring more of those cinnamon rolls?"

Bruce laughed. "I'd guarantee it," he said as he waved and watched Toby drive back toward his house.

With his arm around Sarah's shoulders, and hers wrapped tightly around his waist, they walked back to the house in silence.

Once inside, she walked him to the kitchen where he sat down in one of the kitchen chairs and she busied herself getting him a glass of water and an ice pack.

"You're beautiful," he said as she hurried around the kitchen.

"Shut up. Just shut up." Tears streamed down her cheeks. "Here." She set the glass on the table and pressed the ice pack to the back of his head and he winced.

"Thank you." He moved his hand to hold the ice pack.

"I need to find my keys. We need to get you to a doctor."

"Let's talk."

Sarah's nostrils flared as she sucked in air and studied him. "Talk? You want to talk? You said you needed a doctor," she yelled over the music still playing.

"I do. We'll get to that."

Then, as if all of her energy had been used, she fell into the chair next to him, before standing and turning off the music that she must have finally realized was blaring in the background.

"What are you listening to?" he asked on a laugh.

"Speed death metal, or something like that."

"That's your music of choice?" The thought humored him.

"It is when I'm pissed off and cleaning. Besides, no one lives around here, and Toby can't hear it from the house. So…"

"So you opened all the windows and had yourself a pity party?"

Her shoulders dropped as she sat down in the chair again. "I guess I did."

"And what happened to make you so mad that you listened to deranged music?"

The smile flirted on her lips before the frown took over. "We're going to talk about my music? You fainted in the driveway and hit your head. We should be going to the damned hospital!" she shouted.

Bruce took her hand. "I'm fine. Trust me. Now why are you pissed?"

"Alex came to see me at work today."

"Oh."

"He doesn't want us living together."

"No surprise."

"And I told him I love you."

Bruce lowered the ice pack and then put it on his elbow. "You told him that?"

"He needs to know."

"And his head is still attached?"

She chuckled. "Yeah. He's not happy."

"I don't suppose he is."

Sarah took Bruce's hand and interlaced their fingers. "He kept telling me I didn't know you. But I've known you my whole life. I know exactly what you're about."

Bruce swallowed hard. "That's all he told you?"

"I think he wanted to say more, but he didn't."

Well, that was a surprise. The two women closest to Alex didn't know Bruce's secrets because Alex still held on to them. Why he was being such an asshole was beyond Bruce, but wasn't it interesting that Alex was keeping his promise through it all to never tell a soul what he knew?

"So?" Sarah drew his attention back to her. "What secret is my brother keeping that he won't tell me?"

Bruce lifted his hands to Sarah's cheeks and held her, much as his grandmother had earlier that morning. "I have a lot to tell you."

"Then tell me. I won't stop loving you."

And he wasn't sure of that.

"I have to go slow."

"Why?"

"There isn't just one part. But I'm going to tell you what happened out there and why I have this goose egg on my head. Then, we're going to call Rachel."

Her eyes narrowed on him. "Why Rachel?"

"I said I needed a doctor, and I'm going to need her."

CHAPTER 21

Sarah sat in the chair next to Bruce as he adjusted the ice pack from his elbow back to his head.

When she'd said he needed a doctor, she certainly didn't assume he needed a therapist.

Now the little bits her brother had let out scared her. If she didn't know him, who was he?

"Should I call Rachel now?" she asked.

He looked at his watch, and then back at her. "If you want to. If she's not busy, it would take her an hour or so to get here."

"And if I wait?" Her voice shook.

"Then she'll come later. I'm not going to do anything, Sarah. I'm not going to hurt you."

"I'm not worried about me."

And he took that as a huge compliment. "I'm not going to hurt me either."

"Why do you need Rachel and not a doctor? You hit your head. You just collapsed out there."

Bruce gathered her hands and placed a kiss to her fingers. "I got triggered when I pulled up. And, I guess that's how I reacted.

I'm going to let you in on some of what your brother is trying to warn you about. I'll need Rachel when I'm done."

Sarah's heart was racing so fast she wondered if it might leap from her chest. He was scaring the hell out of her, but she wasn't afraid. She needed to tell him that. So why wouldn't the damn words surface?

Bruce smiled. "You look petrified. Maybe we should go to your brother's. Or somewhere public."

"Why would we do that?"

"I don't want you to be afraid of me."

"I'm not."

"You're shaking." He said as he let go of her hands and she saw that she was. "Do you trust me?"

"Of course I do."

"Then call Rachel and see if she can come here. If she can't leave the baby, maybe we can go there."

"Bruce, you're really scaring me. I'm not afraid of you. I'm afraid for you."

He nodded. "I've been through this many times. Call Rachel."

Sarah stood, retrieved her phone, and walked out to the front porch.

She needed a moment to think, and a moment to calm herself.

Pushing the contact name, Rachel's face popped up and a few moments later Rachel's voice gleefully rang out.

"I need your help," Sarah said and she heard the fear in it.

"God, Sarah, what's wrong?"

"I don't know," she began as she sat down in one of the rocking chairs on the front porch. "It's not me. It's Bruce. He needs you. He asked for you."

"You're scaring me. You're okay?"

"I'm fine," she said and then the tears started again. "I'm fine. Something is wrong with him."

"Craig should be home in a few minutes. I'll head to you. Where are you?"

Sarah took a breath. "We moved into the guest house behind Toby's."

"Who is we?"

"Me and Bruce."

"You're living together? You're together? Sarah, I'm missing pieces."

The sobs were coming harder now. Of course she was missing pieces because they'd been keeping the whole thing quiet. But it wasn't quiet anymore.

"Yes, you are. But get here. Help him and I'll tell you everything you're missing."

She could hear movement on the other end and she knew Rachel was getting herself together to hurry to them. "I'll be there in an hour. If you don't feel safe, you call 9-1-1."

"Why wouldn't I feel safe?"

"I don't know, because I don't understand why you're calling me."

"He needs you."

"Okay," Rachel said. "I'll be there for him. I'll always be there for him."

BRUCE SIPPED ON THE WATER AND BREATHED IN AND OUT, JUST AS he'd been trained to do since he was a young boy. He closed his eyes and went to his happy place.

It had changed over the years. At first it was his bedroom in his mother's house. He'd picked out the comforter and the wallpaper. She'd let him keep the night light on, and he could always walk down the hall and climb into her bed. She allowed him to do that.

When he'd been pulled from under that bed, and the comforter, sheets, wallpaper, and all of his toys had been left behind, he picked a new happy place.

At first it was his grandparents' car, because they went on adventures in that car.

In time, it became his car, then his house. It had moved to championship games in college, and pretty girls. But for the longest time, his happy place had been anywhere Sarah was. And now, he needed to guide himself to his happy place, even though it was in turmoil.

"She's on her way," Sarah's voice broke through the silence and he opened his eyes. "What do you need?"

"I need you to not be afraid."

"I'm not."

"You're still shaking and now you're crying."

She studied him before taking the chair in front of him and moving it away slightly before she sat down.

That was fine. He wasn't going to hurt her and she was about to find that out.

"I want you to know that at any point when I tell you this part of my story, and you want to walk away, you do it. Whether it be away from the story, or me forever, I'll understand."

"Why did you collapse, Bruce? If there is something wrong with you, maybe we can get it fixed."

He smiled. "I'm fixed, honey. I've been fixed for years. But just like a heart that has been replaced or a limb that has been removed, there are still challenges. When I heard you scream, it just hit me a little hard."

"Why?"

"I'll tell you."

CHAPTER 22

The words to the story hadn't been said aloud, in order, in nearly twenty years. There had been pieces and parts told to therapists, and Alex, but he never told the story in order. And he wasn't going to tell her all of it. Not now.

He'd talk until Rachel arrived, and then he'd owe Rachel the story too.

"When I pulled up I could hear the music. I was laughing because it's horrible music."

"It diverts my anger," she told him.

"It's good to know. I'll make wise choices when I hear you playing it again." He rubbed his hands together. "My mother loved music. She liked Harry Connick Jr. best. She'd play it when she was cooking. And then after dinner, when she was cleaning, before my dad would go out for his shift, they'd dance in the kitchen."

Bruce noticed her knuckles had gone white from gripping her hands together in her lap. He wouldn't reach for her. He didn't want to scare her, but it was inevitable.

"Anyway, your music hit me first, but it was your scream that rattled me to my bones."

"I hate mice."

He chuckled. "I'm not fond of them either. But it was the scream, that scared, blood curdling scream that triggered my paralyzing memory."

"I'm so sorry."

Bruce held up his hand. "Don't be. You don't get to say you're sorry for anything where this is concerned. Deal?"

She nodded, but he was sure he'd hear the word a few more times.

"You screamed and it made me think of my mother." He took a moment and a cleansing breath. "I was ten. She was thirty. She loved flowers in vases on the kitchen table, walks through the park where she'd let me play on the playgrounds, and Rocky Road ice cream. Her hair was the color of spun gold, and her eyes were this crystal blue that I've never seen anyone else have. Her pinkie on her right hand was crooked."

Bruce held up his hand and looked at his own crooked pinkie.

"We shared that," he said. "My favorite book was Huck Finn. The part where they're painting the fence, that just stuck with me for some reason."

Sarah's shoulders eased, and it gave him some calm.

"We had fish sticks for dinner. She made her own tartar sauce. On that night we actually had french fries, but had dad been home for dinner, it would have been vegetables. He thought she needed to give me more vegetables."

Sarah wiped her hands on the legs of her pants. Bruce was sure the blood had been drained from them and she was trying to regain feeling. But he'd continue.

"We watched a rerun of I Love Lucy on TV before I was supposed to go to bed. Dad had pulled a double that day, so he wasn't home for dinner."

Bruce ran his hand over his hair and closed his eyes.

"It was an apartment," he remembered. "Third floor, second door from the stairwell. It was tiny."

When he opened his eyes she was watching him intently.

"Mom had tucked me into bed and then she went out to the kitchen to clean up dinner."

Bruce picked up the water and sipped. His throat was going dry, and he wasn't even sure he could get through the next part of the story. Putting the events in order was draining him.

"At some point I heard loud voices. They were my parents' voices. Dad had come home and they started to argue. I remember him saying, 'What did you tell them?' over and over again." He wiped his hand over his face.

"Who was them?" Sarah finally spoke and it drew Bruce out of his head for just a moment.

"The police."

She sat back in her chair and nodded, as if it were okay for him to go on.

"She kept denying that she'd told anyone anything. When I opened my door, I saw him shove her up against the counter. Her head hit the cabinet, and then he punched her. I didn't do anything. I should have saved her."

"You were ten."

"I was her entire life. I needed to be her savior," he said as he wiped the fresh tears that rolled down his cheeks, then he closed his eyes. "He grabbed her by her hair and pulled her through the kitchen. She was bleeding from her nose and crying. She was crying," he repeated.

Sarah took his hand, and he opened his eyes. She was still there and now she'd reached for him. It was more than he could have asked for.

"Then he took the knife off the counter and she let out that blood curdling scream."

"Oh, Bruce."

"I watched my father knock my mother to the ground, straddle her, and plunge a knife into her chest, over and over again. Then he took the knife and went straight across her throat."

Sarah's sobs pulled him out of his story, and she moved to him, wrapping her arms around him and holding his head against her chest.

Still sitting in the chair, he wrapped his arms around her and sobbed.

Why was it as vivid twenty-two years later? Why couldn't he forget it? Why couldn't he just go to his happy place and stay there forever?

They both heard the car pull up out front. "She must have made it past every cop in town with a radar gun," Bruce joked knowing that Rachel had sped to get to them.

When the door opened, he heard footsteps that didn't belong to any woman. Behind him stood Alex, fists clenched to his side.

"What are you doing here?" Sarah asked first.

"Craig called and said Rachel was on her way. That something was wrong. I just needed to know he hadn't touched you."

Bruce closed his eyes and tried to pull up a happy place. He wasn't going to belt his best friend right across the mouth for that, but he wanted to. He wanted to real bad.

CHAPTER 23

Sarah moved to her brother, her hands coming up to his chest, pushing him back.

"That asshole part of you is seriously coming out hard lately," she said as Alex stumbled back.

"I want to make sure he didn't touch you."

"He's touched me plenty and never hurt me. So back off."

Bruce stood and turned toward them. Alex firmed his stance as if he were ready for a fight.

Sarah stood between them. "You need to both just stand down."

Alex carefully watched Bruce. "So why is Rachel coming?"

"I need her help," Bruce admitted.

"Why?"

"I got triggered. And I'm man enough to ask for help when I need it."

Alex's fists still balled at his side. "What triggered you?"

Bruce nodded toward Sarah. "She did."

Sarah's hands were still on her brother's chest. "I'm going to assume you know this story. So you need to just stand down and be calm."

Alex took his sister's hands off his chest, and moved so that she was behind him, as if he were protecting her. "So what did you do to her?"

Bruce stepped closer to them. "I didn't do anything to her. I told her about the night my father killed my mother."

Alex ran his hands over his hair. "And that triggered you?"

Bruce shook his head, and there was the slightest glimmer of humor in his eyes. "No, that wasn't it. She screamed at a mouse."

Alex blinked hard twice before shaking his head. "Can I talk to you? Outside?"

Sarah shook her head. "I don't think that's a good idea. I think you should just go home," she said.

"I'm not going anywhere," Alex argued.

The front door opened again and Rachel ran into the house scanning a look over Alex. "What are you doing here?"

"Craig called and said something was wrong."

She tightened her jaw and pursed her lips. "Damnit. I told him not to do that."

"Well, he must have thought something was wrong." Alex turned back to his sister. "Just like I do."

"Well, maybe you're both assholes," Sarah said taking a step back toward Bruce.

Rachel stepped between them. "Are you okay?" She asked Bruce. "Sarah couldn't tell me much."

Bruce smiled. "I'm okay. Thank you for coming."

"I'm sure there has to be someone better suited..."

"You're the perfect person," he assured her with that calm tone that could put them all at ease. "There is a nice porch out back with a fireplace, gas of course. Why don't we go out there, if you don't mind?"

Rachel nodded and shifted a glance between him and Alex. "I'll follow you outside."

Bruce smiled at Rachel then turned his gaze to Sarah. He was hurting deep inside, but she knew he was in good hands, and that was what he was trying to tell her when he looked at her.

Before they walked out of the kitchen, he shifted one more look toward Alex, and Sarah understood that one to be a warning, which Alex seemed to heed.

Sarah watched the man she loved walk out of the house with Rachel, though it wasn't just Rachel the friend, this was Rachel the therapist and she was there to help someone in need.

Alex ran his hands over his hair again and paced a small circle in the living room.

Sarah watched him pace. The small bit of information Bruce had shelled out wasn't the whole story, and her brother apparently knew the whole story.

"What hasn't he told me yet?" she asked.

Alex lifted his head and shook it. "I gave him my word."

"So as a brother and a best friend, you still hold him in high regard and will keep his secrets?"

"Until he tells me otherwise."

"Yet you will stand here and threaten him, worried that he might hurt me?"

"Yes."

"None of this makes sense to me," she said.

Alex pulled her in and held her. "When he tells you all of it, it will make sense. My side and his side."

"I love him," she said.

"So do I, and I still don't want you with him."

RACHEL SAT DOWN IN THE CHAIR THAT WAS OFFERED TO HER AND Bruce started the fireplace.

"I want you to know I appreciate you coming out here," he said as the fire roared to life. "Can I get you anything?"

"I'm fine."

"I also want you to know that I understand the traumas you've gone through. I was there for them. I worked through them with my therapists as they happened to you. And I'd understand if you walk out. I won't hold it against you. I won't think of you less as a friend, or a professional."

Rachel crossed her legs and placed her hands on her knee, just as his grandmother had done that morning. "I'm here as a friend, first and foremost."

"I appreciate that."

"Why don't you tell me your story?"

Bruce let out a breath and took the other chair. "What do you know about my past? It'll give me a good place to start."

"What I know is you grew up with Alex. I think you went to some snotty private school."

That made him laugh. "Man, if the kids I knew back in Chicago could have seen me in my uniform. But yeah, you're right."

"I know your grandparents raised you."

"Okay."

"And I know your mom died, and you didn't have any other relatives because your father was in jail."

"Where he'll be for two hundred and thirty-six years," he confirmed.

Her eyes went wide, for just a beat, and then her calm and collected mannerisms returned.

"That's a mighty long time."

"Sure is. Without the same detail I gave Sarah, when I was ten, I watched my father brutally murder my mother."

And he'd surprised her.

Rachel's hand went to her chest, her mouth opened, and she gasped. She wasn't the first professional to have that expression, but he knew it was his friend that had reacted.

"Bruce, I had no idea."

"No one did."

"For some reason I thought she died of cancer or something, and as luck would have it, your dad was in jail."

He couldn't help but smile at that. "It's interesting what people must think. Then again, when I moved in with my grandparents, that's all we told people. Actually, we only told people that my mom died and my dad wasn't in the picture."

"No one would question that."

"Very few. I got some sympathy, but for the most part, it sounded as normal as possible."

Rachel reached for his hand and held it between hers. "What made you tell her all of this today?"

"There was an interesting series of events, and it appears that when I hear the woman I love scream like she's being attacked, I pass out."

"She screamed?"

"There was a mouse."

Rachel laughed, and reeled it back in. "Sorry, that wasn't funny."

"In hindsight it's hysterical."

"But it triggered that specific memory?"

"Yeah."

"Remember, Craig split his head open on a rock when he'd heard I got shot. You big macho guys…"

"We have a soft side."

"And that's why I love you both."

CHAPTER 24

*R*achel let go of his hand and eased back in her chair. "Do you mind me asking you about you and Sarah?"

"What do you want to know?"

"When did that all start? I assume it started and that's why Alex has been acting so strange."

Bruce rested his forearms on his thighs and leaned in. "New Year's Eve, officially. We had a bit too much to drink, and apparently were making out at Toby's party."

"I missed all the good stuff that night."

"You gave birth to the most beautiful girl. You didn't miss a thing," he reminded her.

"You're right. It turned out the be the best New Year's Eve for me too." She clasped her hands in her lap. "So you got together?"

Bruce shrugged. "We let it slide. You know, we'd always wanted to do it. It was a dream come true. But Alex forbade it."

"Now that you say that, I've heard him tell you that for years. I just thought it was a brotherly thing because you had a thing for his sister."

"I thought that too. Then we crossed the line at Kelly and

Ray's wedding, and when she asked me to live with her in her new townhouse, that's when Alex started becoming more aggressive with forbidding me."

"That's what that was about at the YMCA?"

"Yeah. He didn't even know I'd snuck Sarah home and to bed with me," he said smiling.

"You snuck Alex's sister into his house and had sex in your apartment?"

"I did."

"Damn, you're lucky to be alive."

"I love her."

Rachel's eyes went wide, and then moist. This was no longer the therapist in front of him. This was his friend. "You love her?"

"I've loved her for years. The bonus, come to find out, she had feelings for me too."

"This whole time?"

"Yep. We just skirted around it because of Alex."

Rachel shook her head. "That's unfortunate."

"It is, but I understand it now. It became very clear the other day when I skipped out on the game, after an innocent conversation with Sarah stirred up old feelings, Alex loves me and he loves her. He just doesn't want a man who has the blood of a serial killer running through his veins sleeping with, and falling in love with his sister."

Rachel let out a long, slow breath. "Whoa. You just unloaded a lot of stuff right there," she said leaning in toward him. "Your dad killed your mom."

"Yeah."

"And they caught him?"

"Took him out of the kitchen, right over her dead body. The neighbors had called when they heard her scream."

"You don't get two hundred and thirty-six years for killing your wife. You should, but it doesn't happen. Bruce, what else did he do?"

She was right. He'd unloaded a lot in that one sentence. "He terrorized Chicago. He kidnapped, raped, and brutally killed eight other women."

Both of her hands came to her mouth now. "Bruce..."

"Don't say you feel sorry for me. I have been in counseling since I was ten. That's why I say I went through all your trauma with you. I took it to my sessions and we worked through it too. That's why I want you here. You understand that I'm okay. You're okay. We just have things. And sometimes we have to rework those things."

"And we never know when they'll rise up, yank us by the ankles, and pull us under water."

"Yes."

"I will forever have guilt knowing you had to work through my trauma."

"I'd be disappointed if you did. I know what it is to see someone you love lying there dead and you can't do anything but step over them to free yourself. The moment you found your brother, I called my therapist and told her about it. It wasn't so much that it was making me relive it, I wanted to know what to do to help you."

"Bruce..."

"And when I'd heard that you were cutting yourself and tried to commit suicide too, I had to ask questions. I had to understand it. I needed to know that bad things happen to us, but we don't have to continue the bad."

"And when I was shot?"

Bruce took her hands in his. "I sat at the hospital and waited for word. Then I went to the chapel and prayed, even though I don't believe in God."

"Why would you?"

She understood.

"I took it to my therapist and we walked through you helping that boy and him dying and you getting shot. I prayed for your baby, that you wouldn't lose her. The universe heard my prayers."

"Do you ever feel as if you could hurt someone?" she asked and Bruce shook his head.

"I get angry, and I process it. I've been taught how. I get low, blue, sad, you name it. I work through it. I call my therapist. I visit my grandmother."

"But now you have Sarah."

Bruce smiled. "Now I have Sarah. I have a lot more to tell her."

"She doesn't know about the other women your dad killed?"

"Not yet. And, even though he's decided to be the biggest asshole in history, Alex is still holding my secret."

"He hasn't told anyone?"

"No. Not Catherine. Not Sarah. He swore he never would."

"I think it's safe to say he's still on your side."

Bruce let go of her hands and eased back in his chair. "I need him fully on my side. I'm not my father. I will never be my father. I've worked very hard to train myself to be calm, thoughtful, and to seek help when I need it."

"Like tonight?"

"She scared the shit out of me," he admitted. "When I heard her scream, I just blacked out. She asked if I wanted a doctor, and I said I wanted you."

"That's quite an honor."

"Well now there are two of you that know most of the truth about what brought me to Colorado. Sarah knows some. The only people who know it all are my grandparents."

"I'd be even more honored if you shared with me."

"I think I just might. In time. But what I need from you is help letting Alex know that I'm okay. And Sarah is going to be okay."

"I can tell him my side."

"Rach, Alex loved you and cared enough to go to you in your moment of need way back when Craig left and you needed help. I can guarantee your word will be good with him."

"He's still going to put up a fight."

"I expect it, and I'm okay with sending Sarah home with him for the night. It won't be forever. Like I said, I love her."

CHAPTER 25

*S*arah paced in her brother's small kitchen while he poured them each a glass of whiskey.

"This is stupid. I should be at home with him. He needs me," Sarah said when Alex handed her a glass.

"This was his idea."

"Because, and I repeat, you're an asshole."

Alex shook his head. "I'm an asshole who loves my sister and my best friend. And I happen to worry about both of you. I worry that something inside of him will snap. How do I live with myself when that snap happens and I lose you?"

Sarah sipped her whiskey and her hands shook. "I don't think that anything is going to happen."

"I can't believe you're sleeping with him," Alex said as he lifted his glass to his lips.

"It's love."

"Is it?"

She sighed. "It is."

Alex leaned up against the counter. "I want to be happy for you both. Deep down inside, I want to be happy."

"Then do."

Alex sipped his drink again and sucked in a breath when it burned. "We were seventeen when he told me where his dad was. Or, why he was where he was."

"You didn't know before that?"

"I knew his mom was dead. He lived with his grandparents. And at some point, I think it was in ninth grade, when someone asked him where his parents were, he blurted out something like, my dad is in jail."

"Did anyone believe him?"

Alex laughed and shook his head. "No. They all figured he was a big fat liar who shoplifted cigarettes."

"He what?"

Alex pulled out a chair from the kitchen table and sat down. "I'm not the one to tell you all of this. You don't realize how big a six year age gap is until you face the things you did at sixteen, and your sister was only ten."

"Trust me I get it. Because in your eyes, I'll always be ten." Sarah pulled out a chair and sat down. "But, Alex, I'm sleeping with your best friend."

He groaned. "There's part of me that thinks I'm going to vomit when you say that."

Catherine walked into the kitchen, placing a hand on Sarah's shoulder as she passed through. "You're not going to vomit. If you were a good brother, you'd let her give you all the yummy details," she said as she opened the refrigerator and pulled out the orange juice.

"She was the woman in the basement after the wedding. That's enough yummy details for me," he said.

Catherine pulled a glass from the cupboard. "I know she was." She winked at Sarah. "And she's in love."

Sarah raised her brows. "See, she gets it."

Alex finished his whiskey and worried his bottom lip. "The only person who doesn't get it is you," he spat out the words as he stood and walked out of the kitchen. A moment later the bedroom door closed.

Catherine poured the juice into the glass, and replaced the bottle in the refrigerator. "I still don't understand why he's so worried," Catherine said as she picked up her glass, sat down in the chair Alex had occupied, and sipped.

"You don't know what Alex does?"

She shook her head. "I know Bruce's dad is in jail and his mom died, that's why he lived with his grandparents."

"Alex didn't say anything else to you?"

"He didn't even tell me that," she admitted. "That much seemed to be common knowledge."

Sarah nodded. Even she had known that much. There was some respect to be given to her brother. That was a sign of a true friend.

Catherine sipped her juice. "Do you want to tell me all about it?"

Sarah studied her sister-in-law. What would it hurt if she told her what she and Alex both knew?

Then again, only she, Alex, and Rachel knew the truth. It was a heavy burden, but at the same time, it was an amazing gift.

"Please don't think I'm being rude by not telling you," she said.

Catherine reached her hand to cover Sarah's. "I don't think you're rude. I think that's amazingly sweet. But, even though I don't know all the details, know that I'm on Bruce's side. I want the best for him and for you. I'm glad that you're in love. It feels so good, doesn't it?"

Sarah smiled. "It does. I always wished for it. I didn't think it would ever happen."

"Oh, anyone who saw the two of you knew. Trust me."

BRUCE SAT ON HIS COUCH IN THE DARK, WITH ONLY THE FLICKER OF the TV illuminating the room. He'd pulled a bottle of beer out of the refrigerator, but left it unopened.

Somewhere between Sarah leaving and the moment he sat down with the beer, he'd decided that it was one more crutch, and tonight, he needed to feel all the feels.

Rachel had offered him the support he'd needed. Though, her professionalism was often trumped by personal feelings for him, he was comfortable telling her what he had. Of course, he hadn't shared it all, but in time, they were all going to need to know.

Alex had proved to him that his friends could keep his secrets. Maybe the rest of the world didn't need to know, but his dearest friends—his family—needed to know.

There was the inevitable. His grandmother wouldn't be around much longer. If he was really lucky, he'd have another decade, but with his grandfather already gone, he knew the day would come for his grandmother too. Then, his friends would be his only family—his chosen family, just as his grandparents were.

And, of course, if things were going to move forward with Sarah, he had a lot more secrets to tell her. Hopefully, if given in little doses, it would give her time to absorb them.

He sunk in his seat, and turned the channel with the remote.

Bruce missed her. He'd needed to send her to Alex's for the night for her own good, and Alex's peace of mind. But the night was going to be long and lonely.

As he flipped through the channels, his father's face flashed on the screen. Bruce turned back and watched the thirty second ad about serial killers, and the one episode that focused on his father.

Bruce felt his hands start to shake as they flashed the pictures of the eight women they would eventually find, and then focused on a picture of his mother.

Bruce paused the TV.

He missed her. He missed her something awful.

After years of therapy, he'd been taught to focus on the happy times he had with his mother—and there were many happy times.

As he studied his mother's face, frozen in time, he pressed a kiss to his fingers and blew it in her direction.

Now that the documentary was ready to air, the rest of his story needed to come to light among his friends. His anonymity would forever be intact among them, and that was all that mattered—that and the memory of his mother.

CHAPTER 26

*G*ray clouds rumbled above Bruce as he pulled his gym bag from his car. The regular Sunday basketball game was down a player with Toby out of town, but they usually figured it out.

Bruce scanned the lot for familiar cars. Craig and Rachel were already there. Ray's mini-van was parked closer to the door, which meant the kids were in tow. Alex's car was a few rows away. But the car he didn't see was Sarah's.

He hadn't seen her since Wednesday, when he'd sent her to stay with Alex. Maybe that had been a mistake. They'd talked on the phone, but she hadn't come back to Toby's.

Taking a deep breath, he promised himself not to read too much into it. They were all busy. Had they not moved into Toby's together, chances were he wouldn't have seen her all week anyway.

Usually he'd assume the worst, and then the worst would happen. He'd assume she was mad or over him, and in actuality she was just busy. So, he was just going to go with that thought— she was busy. He knew in his heart he missed her desperately, so hopefully she missed him too.

"You look lost, sailor," her voice came from behind him.

When he turned, she walked toward him. Her long legs exposed from a pair of red shorts. The tank top she wore showed off her sculpted shoulders. Her dark hair was pulled back in a ponytail, but the smile she wore was sexy enough to jump start the heat in his body.

"Man, you're a sight for sore eyes," he said as she moved to him, immediately wrapping her arms around his neck. "I've missed you."

"It's only been a few days," she said lightly.

"Four. It's been four days."

Sarah pressed a kiss to his lips. "The townhouse is ahead of schedule. I'll close in two weeks."

"That's good news."

"And I still want you to come with me."

There was a heaviness in his body. "What does Alex say about that?"

"I don't care what Alex has to say about that."

"You're not afraid of me?"

Sarah pressed her forehead to his. "I've never seen you be violent, even when you could have been. I'm not afraid of you."

"I am."

Sarah eased back. "I guess we should work on that."

"I've worked on it my entire life. But now I have you and I'm more scared than ever."

"I love you. We all have flaws, your father's aren't yours."

And that was the nicest thing anyone had ever said to him, he thought. "I don't want to cause problems between you and your brother."

Sarah shrugged. "I think the relationship between me and my brother is strong enough to handle this. He loves you too."

"I know. I just don't want to hurt any of you."

"Then don't." She pressed a kiss to his lips. "Let's go kick their asses. You and I against the three of them. It should be a fair game."

THE GAME ENDED UP BEING MORE FUN THAN HE COULD HAVE imagined. Ray's kids, Connor and Charlotte, teamed with Bruce and Sarah. Luckily, everyone was in the mood that anything could go, and Connor thought that was the way to go.

When Bruce picked him up and flew him to the net for a slam dunk, the crowd went wild, or so it felt when Kelly stood and cheered her son, and his father scooped him up and placed a noisy kiss to the top of his head.

Bruce watched in awe. His life had been so different, but he didn't begrudge anyone who had what Connor and Charlotte had. He'd had some of that until he was ten, it just became very marred when he found out who his father really was, but by that time his mother was gone.

Craig's hand came to his shoulder. "You're deep in thought."

"I sure am."

"They're great kids. It's cool to think that all of our kids will grow up together too."

The statement was innocent enough, and Bruce simply nodded. He supposed he'd better flip the thought into something positive rather quickly. Okay, he'd always be Uncle Bruce, and they'd adore him.

Then he looked at Sarah. Maybe they should have that talk sooner than later. What if it was a deal breaker? He may never even have to tell her what his father did if she walked away because he'd made himself sterile.

Charlotte ran across the court with the ball between her hands.

"My turn," she said looking up at Bruce.

The bubble of joy that lodged in his chest brought a smile to his face, especially when he looked toward Sarah, who leaned up against Charlotte's father Ray, her arm casually on his shoulder.

Bruce picked up Charlotte, her squeal of delight resonating in his ear.

He flew her across the court and to the basket, letting her hang from the hoop for just a moment, until she dropped right in his arms.

Again, the loud celebration erupted for the preschooler, and Bruce felt the cloud that had been shrouding him for days lift.

Alex placed a hand on his shoulder. "Everyone is talking about brunch. You in?"

Bruce couldn't help but take a moment to study his dear friend. There was a hesitation that reached his eyes, but Bruce knew deep down it wasn't a feeling that Alex wanted to have.

"Are you sure you want me to go?"

Alex nodded. "You're going to take care of her, right? I can't lose my sister. Metaphorically or literally."

"I love her."

"You always have," Alex agreed.

"Always."

Alex put his arm around Bruce's shoulders. "I'm not okay with this. I've spent the better part of twenty years not wanting it. But I'm married to a woman who used to think I was a douchebag, so I get it. Things aren't always what they seem."

That brought a laugh to Bruce. "I'm exactly who I seem, and who you've always known me to be. Give me another chance."

"Just take care of her."

CHAPTER 27

Sarah had come back to him with her brother's understanding, even if he didn't like the idea. For the next two weeks, they'd re-formed a little routine in the guest house behind Toby's.

There were kisses good morning, coffee shared on the way out, and dinners together when they came home. Rachel, Catherine, and Kelly had invited Sarah to their nacho and margarita Thursday nights, and with Toby back in town, guys' night was back on in Toby's game room.

Things felt normal again, and Bruce would never take that for granted again.

When he walked into Toby's basement, Connor and Charlotte ran past him with pool noodles.

Ray shook his head. "They begged to come."

"I like when they're here," Bruce admitted. "Charlotte didn't want to do girls' night?"

Ray laughed. "It's too serious. All the girls do is talk. We play."

"Sounds better to me, too," he admitted.

He helped himself to a beer from behind Toby's bar. "Where is everyone else?"

"Alex is on his way. Craig and Toby are in the media room watching something, but the kids are running amuck, so I'm out here."

"Game of pool?"

"Get ready to lose," Ray said as he walked toward the table and began racking the balls. "So, Alex finally gave you his blessing to sleep with his sister?"

Bruce looked around for the kids, but realized they weren't around and that's why Ray had asked. "He just isn't currently threatening me. Let's put it that way."

"I would think that having his best friend be his sister's lover would be ideal."

"Think that over. Alex knows everything about me. I get why he would be apprehensive."

Ray laughed as he took the first shot. "Solids," he said as he walked around the table and lined up his shot. "I've known you just a few years less than Alex. I'd let you date my sister."

"And you say that because you don't have a sister."

"Maybe. So you smoked some pot. You drank your share." He hit another ball. "You did spend a night in jail, though."

"And because I was being lured in by an underaged girl, whom I never touched, they let me sleep it off and sent me home. That doesn't show on any record, just in the memories of my friends."

"Still stands, man. I'd let you date my sister."

When the ball that Ray was aiming for failed to go into the pocket, Bruce took his shot.

"How are you and Kelly? Things are good?"

Ray leaned a hip against the table. "Better than good. There will never be a day where I don't thank my lucky stars that I convinced her to marry me again. The loss of the baby still hurts. That would have been an amazing blessing, but we have Connor and Charlotte, and each other. The baby would have been perfect, but as Charlotte and Connor have told us, the baby went to be with my dad in heaven, and that seems to bring us all comfort."

"I'm happy for you all—that you're together."

Bruce hit his shot and lined up another. But just as he pulled back his cue to aim, Connor ran out of the media room chasing Charlotte with their pool noodle swords.

He hit her across the back and she went down, then he stood above her and began to pretend to stab her, yelling, "Die!"

Bruce's shot banked off the side of the table and into the floor. Ray, obviously mortified by what his children were doing, lifted his head up to look at Bruce who felt the blood drain from his face.

"What are you two doing?" Ray asked as he pulled Connor from Charlotte just as Alex cleared the basement stairs. "We don't play like that. Where did you see that?"

Connor pointed to the other room. "They're watching it on TV," he said.

It was Alex's eyes that went wide, and without another word he headed into the media room where Craig and Toby sat in the dark.

Ray had the mindfulness to walk his children out of the room and to the patio where they would be out of earshot.

Bruce, lightheaded, followed Alex to the other room.

Alex turned on the lights and took the remote from Toby's hands.

"What in the hell is wrong with you two? What are you watching?" His voice had risen to that seething volume Bruce was used to having aimed at him.

Both Toby and Craig looked up at him with wide eyes.

"What is your problem?" Craig asked as he stood to face off with Alex.

"First of all, those kids were watching this."

Craig and Toby exchanged looks, and Toby stood, taking the remote back. "I'm sorry, man. We didn't know they'd come in here."

"What was that?"

Toby looked up at the blank screen. "It was the serial killer documentary. I recorded it so we could watch it. Dude, it's fascinating."

Alex exchanged glances with Bruce, who knew he was pale, he could feel it in his body, which shook.

"Shit," Alex moved to him. "How much did you see?"

"Don't worry about me."

"If you saw your face, you wouldn't be saying that."

Craig moved to them. "What's going on?"

Which of them were going to talk first? What were they going to say?

Bruce turned from his friends and walked out to the bar. He sat down at one of the stools, clasped his hands, and pressed them to his forehead.

"C'mon," Alex said, "I'll walk you home."

Bruce shook his head. "It's time."

"Not because of this. When you're ready."

Bruce looked at his friend. This was the true friendship he'd counted on forever. Yes, he'd been a shit about the relationship Bruce was having with his sister, but Alex had his back. And he'd known he had when Catherine and Rachel didn't know what had happened to Bruce in the past. Now Rachel knew a bit of it, but it was time to come clean so that nothing came of it.

"It's time," Bruce said.

Alex nodded. "Do you want me to call the girls? Do you need Rachel here?"

Bruce shook his head. "No, but you have to promise me that you trust me. I mean that. Because if I come clean to these asshats, I'll have to come clean with Sarah. She can't find out from anyone else. And I can't guarantee that they won't talk."

"They won't."

Bruce shrugged. "If Ray knows, Kelly deserves to know. What if she doesn't want the kids around me anymore?"

Alex rested his hand on Bruce's shoulder. "That would be a regrettable mistake."

CHAPTER 28

Toby set the media room up with the Marvel movie of Connor's choice—approved by Ray. There had been some popcorn made, and they'd been plied with juice boxes too.

When Ray walked out of the media room, he joined the rest of them at the bar, where Bruce worried over a full beer by peeling the label off.

"So what's going on?" Ray asked. "Why are we hiding my kids? Are we really going to open some whoop-ass on Craig and Toby for watching that gore?" There was a smile on Ray's face, but it quickly diminished. "Seriously, what's up?"

Craig and Toby scanned looks over Bruce and Alex. "Are you two okay?" Craig asked. "I know this whole Sarah thing has put a blemish on the perfect brotherhood, but. . ."

Bruce shook his head and took a moment to look them each in the eye.

Alex had been his brother since he'd been eleven.

Ray and Craig had joined that brotherhood the moment they moved into the room across the hall from them in college.

Toby, though he was originally used for parties, since he was the fancy boy with the single dorm room, he'd become as much a brother as the others.

The five of them should have always been together, and those ten years never should have passed without them gathering once a week, as they did now.

But now was the time to share the deep-seated past that had been hidden most of Bruce's life.

Alex rested his hand on Bruce's shoulder, and it told him he would take the first approach.

"Craig and Toby were in on this a little bit last week, and Ray, I guess you'll catch up quick," Alex started. "As you know, our brother Bruce has been a little out of sorts lately." He gave Bruce's shoulder a squeeze and continued. "That show you were watching hits home a little hard."

Toby shook his head. "Man, I'm sorry."

Bruce nodded. "I know. You didn't know this. You just got to see me flat on my back on the ground when I couldn't handle it."

Ray scanned a look over all of them. "Someone needs to fill me in a bit."

Alex took a moment to go over the events with the mouse and Sarah screaming. And then it was time to dive into specifics.

"Are you okay with me telling them, or do you want to do it?" Alex asked.

"I'd feel better if I didn't have to say it out loud."

Alex nodded. "Bruce's dad is featured in that thing you were watching."

Craig leaned in on the bar. "Are you freaking kidding me. Oh, man, I didn't know."

"It's okay," Bruce said again.

"Do we want to know?"

Bruce shrugged. "If you want to know my story you do. But if you think it'll change who you think I am, it's not going to matter."

"I know who you are," Craig said. "And who brought you into

this world has no bearing on who you are. So you guys just drop it on us and we'll deal with it. But, Bruce, whatever you guys are about to tell us, we've always got your back."

Bruce drew in a long breath. Brothers—that's what they were.

"Bruce came to live with his grandparents, and entered into our lives, mine and Sarah's, when he was eleven," Alex began. "That was shortly after they dragged him out of his bedroom in Chicago after his father murdered his mother."

The eyes of the other men had gone wide, but there were no words, and he'd expected that. What did you say to something like that?

"When his father was being prosecuted for his mother's death, it came out that he had murdered eight other women and buried them in different places."

"The Chicago River killer," Toby eked out the words.

Bruce sat upright on his barstool. "I haven't seen my father or spoken to him since the night I watched him murder my mother."

Craig pinched the bridge of his nose. "You watched him do that?"

"I was standing in my bedroom door."

Craig shook his head. "They must not know that. They didn't mention it in the documentary."

"Well, that's a bonus for me then. It was all over the news back then."

Alex walked around the bar and pulled out a beer for himself. "Now you all know what I've known since we were seventeen, and it makes Bruce here quite vulnerable."

"Thanks for that," Bruce said.

"I mean it in a good way. There's more than just me that knows this now. And I'll beat any of these assholes who wants to take me on over it," Alex confided to all of them. "But with that said, it needs to stay close. Rachel knows some. Kelly will want to know," he said to Ray. "I'll let Catherine in on it, and at least it comes from us. There won't be reason to gossip and second guess it all."

Ray ran his hands over his hair. "This is why you didn't want him with Sarah?"

Alex gave Bruce a sympathetic look. "Yeah."

Bruce pushed away the full beer bottle, sans the label, and looked up at Ray. "I love your kids. I want you to know that. In fact, I love all of your kids," he said to Craig and Alex. "I'm not my father. I'm not violent. I'm not angry. I've worked my entire life to not be him. But I'd understand if you didn't want me around your kids. I'd hate it, but I'd understand it."

Ray shook his head. "My kids are better people with you in their lives."

The statement brought a warmth to Bruce's chest.

"That means a lot to me, it really does."

Craig nodded. "You and Rachel are kindred souls, aren't you?"

Bruce chuckled. "We discussed that."

"She's an amazing mother and she's run the gambit of shitty deals dealt to her. If she can love, have a baby, and continue to aid those who need it, then who am I to say you're less than who I know you to be? My daughter will be just fine with you in her life."

"Thank you."

Alex took a long sip from his beer. "I guess there's just one person left to tell. You have an entire team on your side. Do you want us there?"

Bruce looked each of them in the eye, and in that moment, he knew any one of them would come running to help him.

"I think I'll be okay. She'll come to you if she has a problem with it, I'm sure."

"I'll be here for her, too," Alex agreed, and Bruce knew that he'd never be able to hurt Sarah. She, too, had a team behind her.

CHAPTER 29

*S*arah pulled up to the house. The lights were on and it gave her a warm feel—coming home. It was the perfect end to a perfect night.

It had been wonderful to be invited to nachos and margaritas with the girls. The few times she'd ever been around Rachel and Catherine, when she was younger, she'd always looked up to them. Sarah had always been more comfortable with the guys though. Playing basketball with them was right up her alley. But now—well now she was part of the girls too.

She climbed from her car, retrieving her purse from the passenger seat. A smile formed immediately on her lips when she saw Bruce standing in the door. In each hand he held a glass of wine.

"I didn't expect you to be home yet," she admitted as she walked toward him.

"Here I am."

"You don't know how happy that makes me," she said as she took one of the glasses of wine and pressed a soft kiss to his lips. "I'm glad I don't work tomorrow." She sipped the wine as she walked into the house.

"You're off tomorrow?"

"Every other Friday," she offered. "But after margaritas and now wine, I'll need to sleep in longer."

His eyes were dark, and even though he wore a smile, she wondered what hid behind it.

"Your night with the guys was okay?" she asked.

Bruce sipped his wine. "It was revealing, to say the least."

"And what does that mean?"

Bruce took her hand, interlaced her fingers with his. "I have the fire going in the back. Let's go sit."

"Is everything okay?"

He leaned in and lingered a kiss on her lips. "It will be."

They walked out back and each took a chair which faced the fire. Sarah took another sip of her wine and sat down.

BRUCE SAT DOWN NEXT TO HER, HIS GAZE FOCUSED ON THE FLAMES.

"I've been around you your entire life. There isn't much I don't know," he admitted as the fire flickered in front of him. "I'm hoping that our relationship isn't just a fling. . ."

"Is that what you're thinking? I wouldn't have invited you to live with me if that's what I thought." Her voice had become defensive, and he had to smile. Perhaps it was exactly how he had to hear it said.

"No, no. I think it's much more than that." He lifted his eyes to her now worried ones. "I just think, if we're going to make a life of it, you should get to know me."

"Don't I know you?"

He sipped his wine and let out a long breath as he watched the fire dance again.

"Brett Bennett," he said and took another sip of wine.

"Who is Brett Bennett?"

Turning toward her, he locked eyes with hers. "I am."

Sarah's brows drew together. "I'm confused."

"My birth name was Brett Bennett."

She set her glass on the small table to her side and inched her chair closer to his. "I don't understand. You were born under a different name?"

"Constance and Thomas Griffin are not my biological grandparents."

Her palms pressed together. "Your grandparents?" she asked and he nodded. "They're not your grandparents?" She repeated the question as if she were cementing the knowledge in her own mind.

"They were the foster parents that were called when I was pulled from my home in Chicago and brought to Colorado."

Sarah reached for his hands, gripping them in hers. "The night your father killed your mother?" Her voice shook when she said the words aloud.

He nodded. "Anyway, I want you to know. I'm not who I say I am."

Tears were welling in her eyes, and when she batted her lashes, they fell over her cheeks. "You're exactly the man I know you to be."

"True. But I wasn't born that way." Bruce stroked his thumb over her knuckles. "When the Griffins adopted me, we changed my name to protect me. Actually, they did that before they actually adopted me. Brett Bennett was wiped off the map. No one could find him again."

She wiped at her eyes. "This doesn't change how I feel about you."

"I'm not done."

Sarah eased back in her seat. "Sweetheart, you've told me about your past. I don't blame them for changing your name. And from what I remember of your grandparents, they were kind and attentive people. I've told you, you're not your father."

"All of that is true. And I wish I had a way to introduce you to who my mother was. She was amazing. But I don't even have any pictures of her."

"Bruce. . ."

"It's okay. I long ago came to terms with that. But there's more for me to tell you, and I have to do it now, because you're going to see it. You're going to find out." He squeezed his eyes closed tightly. "And I told the guys."

"Before you told me?"

He nodded as he opened his eyes. "It came up in an unfortunate circumstance." He kissed her fingers. "There's a documentary out about serial killers."

"I saw that."

He lifted his eyes to hers again, only now it were his that wore the worry, he knew. "You watched it?"

She shrugged. "It was on when I was at Alex's. I was awake in the middle of the night. So I turned on the TV."

"And that's what you chose to watch?" he asked, more worried about her mental stability than he was his own.

"It caught my attention. Why are we talking about that?"

"Sam Bennett."

Her eyes shifted as if she were recalling the documentary. And when her eyes went wide, he knew she remembered.

"The Chicago River killer?"

"Yes."

"Bennett?" She pulled free one of her hands, and held it to her lips. "Your father?"

Bruce ran the back of his hand over his damp forehead. "Yes."

He could feel her body shake as he held her hand in his.

"Your father killed eight women?"

"Nine, he did kill my mother."

Her lips trembled now. "He kidnapped them and..."

"Yes," he cut off her next sentence because he didn't want to hear it. "Once they arrested him, he confessed to it."

133

"I don't know what to say." The tears rolled down her cheeks, and her breath came in sobs.

"Say you love me," he begged. "Say that it doesn't change anything. Say you trust me. Say. . ."

Sarah reached for him, cupping his face in her hands. "I love you."

Bruce closed his eyes and absorbed that.

"I do trust you," she added.

He opened his eyes and looked into her terrified eyes.

"I'm scared."

CHAPTER 30

*S*arah's hand still shook in his. Or maybe he was the one shaking. He was scared too, so he couldn't deny her the feelings she was having.

"It's okay. I'm scared too," he admitted. "Though, I haven't been scared in years, I am now."

"Why?" She asked through tears that now cascaded over her cheeks. "He's locked up. He's not coming after you."

"I was never afraid of him, except for those few moments before they broke in the door to take him, and when my mother's body had gone limp." He swallowed hard because his mouth had gone dry. "I've always been more afraid of becoming what he was."

"You're not. I can't say it enough. You're not him."

"I threw you against a tree and you hit your head," he reminded her. "I hurt you."

Sarah blinked as if maybe she'd forgotten about that. "No. That was passion. We were..." she stopped and stood as if she now saw it too. "You didn't mean to hurt me."

"I didn't. I thought it was all in the heat of the moment. But the minute your head hit that tree, it flashed before me that maybe all of his feelings were fueled by passion and lust too. What makes a man do that?"

Sarah raked her fingers through her hair. "What do I do with this? God, Bruce, how did you handle this?"

"I've been in therapy my entire life. And every woman I've ever dated catches wind of that, and they leave. They don't even know why the hell I'm in therapy, and they leave."

"And I hope you know that I think more of mental health than to leave, if you're working through your shit."

"I'd like to think so," he said standing, but keeping his distance. "But this is bigger than a suicidal thought, or mixed emotions on something, or just trying to work through my day to day."

"No, it's not," she countered. "Your day to day is different than most people's. God, no wonder you wanted to talk to Rachel the other night. You two have seen some shit." She picked up her glass and took a long drink.

"I've never been shot."

Sarah blinked twice, hard. "You think she's worse off?"

"Her trauma is different, but in actuality, I feared death for a few minutes. She actually faced it."

SARAH STUDIED HIM IN THE SHADOWS. SOMEONE ELSE'S PROBLEMS were bigger than his.

Didn't that say a lot about him? Didn't that say he'd learned that this trauma wasn't actually his. It totally disrupted his entire life, but it wasn't his. It was forced on him from someone else, and he'd taken steps to not become that person?

Standing before her was the man she loved. The man she'd known since she was six, and never—ever had she seen him lose his temper or get mad. Damn, she'd seen her brother and his friends get in fights all the time, but Bruce was never part of that.

Hell, she'd probably gotten into more hair pulling, and gut punching fights.

He stood in front of her, his hands in his pockets. Was he afraid to touch her?

"Would you have told me this if that documentary hadn't come out?" she asked.

He nodded. "Yes. After I knocked you into the tree, it seemed to stir up the guilt, because I knew I loved you too much to hide who I was from you." He ran his hand over his hair. "And then when I heard you scream. . ."

"I'm sorry about that."

"How were you to know? Girls scream. When I'd walk by a playground, when I was younger, and the girls would let out those screams," he winced, "I'd run and hide. I couldn't do it. I couldn't handle that aspect."

"I'm not a screamer, usually."

"You're a yeller," he humored and a smile formed on his lips, for just a moment. "If we continue on, you have to promise me that if I ever scare you, you have to tell me. And if I ever hurt you, you have to fight. And if I ever snap, you have to fight like hell, even if it means. . ."

"I get it," she said, wrapping her arms around herself. "I get it."

Sarah stood apart from him for another moment and studied him. She'd never seen him look weak, except for the night she'd ushered the mouse out of the house. "You were never mentioned in the documentary."

"I've heard that."

"You didn't watch it?"

He shook his head. "Craig and Toby happened to be watching it and Connor and Charlotte walked in."

Sarah winced. "It's graphic."

"All the more reason I don't want to see it. I lived it. But that's how this all came out with the guys. It was just the right time. But Craig mentioned that they didn't say anything about the son."

"So whoever got you out of there and with your grandparents did right by you."

"I've never been approached. I don't know if my grandparents ever had to protect me further, and I don't want to know. All I know is that from the time I was eleven, I was a Griffin. I was Alex Burke's best friend. I was a normal boy, who got to do normal things. I didn't go to sleepovers or slumber parties because I still had nightmares, but somehow it all worked out."

"You've slept over with me," she said.

"I don't have many nightmares anymore," he admitted. "And, Sarah, you're my safe-haven."

Sarah blew out a breath. That was a lot to take on, but it shouldn't be. Anyone who professed their love to another person should be their safe-haven.

Finally she moved to him, wrapping her arms around him, and hoping like hell that the shaking in her body wouldn't send the wrong signal.

"I love you, Bruce," she whispered in his ear. "I'm going to say the wrong thing, or do the wrong thing, and it's going to affect you."

"Ditto."

"Understood. I don't want to lose you though."

His arms wrapped around her tightly. "I don't want to be lost." He eased back and looked her in the eye. "You're the one that said it. I'm the Bruce you grew up with. I'm the same person. Only now you know almost all of my deep dark secrets."

Sarah bit down on her bottom lip. "Almost all of your secrets?"

CHAPTER 31

*B*ruce dropped his arms and stepped back to pick up his wine glass. He drank down what was left.

"The rest of what I told you shouldn't affect you. I mean, I'm trained to deal with every emotion that comes my way. I've never been violent, and I hope to never be."

"But the next thing you're going to tell me will affect me?"

"It will if you really do love me."

Sarah pulled her hair up with her hands, and let it fall again. "I think we've established that. Now what the hell are you going to tell me that's going to make me change my mind?"

"I want to marry you."

Her eyes went wide. "You want to marry me?"

"I do." He chuckled. "I've always wanted to marry you. Since those nights we sat on your driveway during winter break."

"Then you almost married Mindy?"

He shook his head. "I just thought about it. I didn't even ask her."

"Why would you wanting to marry me, make me want to reconsider? And don't think I'm going to let you get away with that being your proposal, because it sucks."

The humor in that made him smile. "I'll do better than that when the time is right. I promise." He moved back to her and took her hands. "I don't want to spread the genetics of that man. His blood line dies with me."

She studied him. "So you don't want children? Is that what you're telling me."

"Yes. Well, no," he shook his head. "I would love to have children. I think you're one hell of an aunt, and I happen to think that kids love me."

"I think they do."

"But I don't want my own biological children."

Sarah turned from him, picked up her wine, and sipped. "That's a lot."

"It is. And it's non-negotiable. I've already taken care of it. I will never have my own biological children."

Slowly she turned back toward him. "You've already taken care of that?"

"I had a vasectomy when I was twenty-two."

Now she drank down the wine. When it was empty, she stood staring into the glass as if willing it to fill again.

Finally, she set down the glass, paced the small porch, then picked up the glass and went back into the house with it.

When she didn't come right back, Bruce followed her, leaving his empty glass outside.

SARAH FILLED THE GLASS AS FULL AS SHE COULD GET IT. REALIZING there was only a few sips left in the bottle, she lifted it to her lips and drank down what was left.

"Getting drunk isn't going to change what I've done," Bruce said as he entered the kitchen and leaned up against the wall casually.

"It's going to help me get through it tonight," she said as she set down the bottle, perhaps a little too heavy handed.

Steadying the bottle from falling over, she picked up her glass, which sloshed. "I'd say you have no right to make that decision, but damnit, your body, your terms."

"Who knew it was a man's right too, huh?"

"Don't do that. Don't minimize women's rights, too."

"I wasn't," he said as he stood straight. "I'm just saying, I did what I needed to do for myself. And I did it when you weren't in the picture. You would have been sixteen when I made that decision. Never in my wildest dreams would I have imagined that you'd be the one I'd be having this conversation with right now."

"Would it have made a difference?" she asked, wondering if her children would have been more important than anyone else's —maybe Mindy's.

"No. It wouldn't have made a bit of difference." He moved to her, took the wine glass, and set it carefully on the counter. "That man deserved the death sentence, but they didn't give it to him. Perhaps someone should have killed me, too."

She took a breath to argue and he placed a finger to her lips.

"I'm not suicidal. I've never even considered it. I'm just saying, there are nine families out there who lost people and maybe they'd like to know it ended with me."

"No one knows you exist."

"And aren't I lucky?" He ran his hands over her shoulders and down her arms until he captured her hands in his. "I can't be responsible for the possible genetics of that man going back out into the world. What if it skips a generation? What if my son were to," he choked on the words, "just what if? Sarah, what I did will save people. That's how I see it."

"But I will never look into my children's eyes and see you. I won't know that their brilliance comes from you, or their height, or their sincerity."

"And that's why I'm telling you this now. It would crush me if you walked out that door, but I'd understand it. I've prepared for that my whole life."

She moved from him, picked up her wine, and took a long drink. When the wine began to make her head spin, she stopped drinking.

"I want to have a baby."

"And then you should have one."

She batted away tears. "I want to have your baby."

"Any baby you give me will be mine."

"That doesn't make sense."

"Sure it does." He moved toward her, but stopped and leaned up against the counter. "We could adopt. We could use a sperm donor. We could ask our friends."

She stared at him. "Ask our friends? Are you kidding me?"

"I'm just saying. We know them."

"And who would I ask? Ray has other kids. Craig has a baby. I'm not asking my brother."

"That would be a horrible idea," Bruce said, and she realized that the wine was now affecting her.

"And, what, that leaves Toby?"

"What's wrong with Toby?"

"Nothing. Nothing at all." She lifted her hair again and walked toward the living room.

WHEN HE FOLLOWED, SHE WAS WALKING CIRCLES AROUND THE coffee table.

"We could adopt. We could foster. We could give someone a life that they weren't going to get," he offered.

"Someone like you?"

"Maybe." He tossed up his hands. "And maybe, just like your own niece, maybe there is a kind and gentle spirit that just needs a home."

Mentioning Celia Rose had caused her to cry again, so he moved to her.

Alex hadn't known about Celia Rose until the police had

shown up on his doorstep and told him that his daughter was okay, but her mother had been killed in a car accident.

Sarah had gone with Alex to get the baby, and she'd fallen in love with her immediately, and Bruce knew that. It could be the same, he thought.

But of course, maybe they'd get a child who had just watched his mother get murdered.

CHAPTER 32

*I*t was nine-thirty at night. It was dark and the air was chilled.

Sarah sat in her car outside of Constance Griffin's house.

She'd been there hundreds of times as a child. There had been a rope swing in the back yard. One year they'd erected a swimming pool. If she remembered correctly, there had been a trampoline until Bruce had broken his arm.

Lemonade stands were once set up on the sidewalk out front of the house, and Bruce and Alex had built a bike ramp out of dirt in the garden. She might have been six years younger than her brother and his best friend, but sitting there, she realized just how much of her life had been entwined with Bruce's and his family.

Now Sarah sat in her car, afraid to talk to the woman who had invited her to visit.

She wrung her hands together in her lap. She'd been livid with Bruce when he'd called his grandmother. But Sarah had driven right over to her house. Only now she didn't have the courage to get out of the car.

The porch light was on, which meant that Constance Griffin

was waiting for her. And when the front door opened, and the old woman stood on the front porch, Sarah knew she needed to get out.

Slowly she opened the door and stepped out. From the street, Sarah could see the smile on the old woman's face, and she remembered it. Constance Griffin had always had a caring nature, and pretty bandages for scraped knees, she remembered.

"Sarah Burke, you have grown into a beautiful woman," Constance said holding her hands out for Sarah.

When Sarah reached her, she took Constance's hands, and accepted the kisses on her cheeks.

"Oh, my Bruce has had a thing for you for as long as I can remember."

Sarah smiled. "I'm learning that."

"Your family has always been good to him. Come on in. I have apple pie cooling on the counter. Let's have some."

Sarah followed Constance into the house that hadn't changed since Sarah was a little girl. There was comfort in that.

The curtains were the same, though the patterned carpet was now hardwood and the TV was updated and hung on the wall. The kitchen still had the same table, and the lace curtains around the windows were the ones Sarah remembered with the cherries embroidered on them.

"Have a seat. I'll get us all set up," Constance said as she walked through the kitchen using the counters to balance herself.

"Can I help?"

"You're my guest. I want you to be comfortable so we can talk."

Sarah wasn't so sure about that. She was anything but comfortable, and that had nothing to do with the woman cutting the apple pie.

"Bruce says he's moving in with you into your new house."

Sarah wiped her hands on her pant legs. "Yes. That's the plan."

"New love," Constance's voice trailed off. "I remember when I met his grandfather. Love at first sight," she said as she turned with two plates full of pie and slowly carried them to the table. "He was Army. Fit as could be, and so fine," she reminisced.

"I remember him being a very gentle and nice man."

"He was, but he could hold his own in a fight if he needed to," Constance confirmed as she set down the plates.

Carefully, Constance pulled out the other chair, and balanced herself against the table to sit down.

"These old bones take some care," she laughed and then looked at Sarah. "You still play basketball with them, Bruce tells me."

"I do. I've always enjoyed kicking their butts."

Constance laughed. "And I know they don't just let you do that. They're too competitive."

"That's true. I grew up around them. I think that's why I'm better. I had to be better than they were."

"Agreed," Constance said as she took her first bite of pie and Sarah followed. "I assume you're really here to learn about Bruce though. He's told you everything, and you need some assurance?"

Sarah had lifted her fork to her lips and then stopped before taking the bite. She lowered her fork back to the plate. "Yea, ma'am. He's told me everything. And I mean everything—I think."

"About Chicago?"

"Yes?"

"You know his name?"

"Yes."

"You know what happened that night, after, and who his father is?"

"Yes, ma'am."

Constance put her fork into a piece of apple and ate it. "You know who I am then?"

"Yes."

"Alrighty. It appears that you are the woman he trusts most in the world, well that is next to me."

Sarah smiled though there were tears stinging her eyes. "It's a lot to take in. I mean, who goes through that?"

"People like Bruce do. There's a lot of killers out there, and some of them have children."

Sarah really hadn't considered that, but his grandmother was right. "He told me he made it so he wouldn't—have children that is."

Constance nodded. "Do you blame him?"

"No. I'm sure he gave that a lot of thought, and I suppose I'm being petty and woeful for myself," which made her feel worse as she heard herself say the words.

"You should mourn that. You'll never have his baby, in that sense."

"And that hurts."

"Of course. But, honey, there a millions of babies who need good mamas and daddies. And there is nothing stopping you from giving birth to a baby. There are ways."

Bruce had brought that up, and she was going to have to consider that—in time.

"Was it hard to raise someone else's child? Especially one that went through what he did?"

Constance put down her fork. "I'd lost so many babies, I didn't want to try anymore. My body wasn't made for giving birth. So we fostered for years, and those babies and children just kept getting taken away. Sometimes they'd send them back to the parents that abused them."

Constance picked up a napkin from the holder on the table and wiped her lips. "One day they called and said they had Bruce. They told us what he'd been through, and I knew I had to protect him. I had to wrap my arms around that boy and hold him—I just knew I did."

"How was he?"

"Scared. Skinny." She used the napkin on her eyes, and wiped away tears that had formed. "By then we were too old to be new parents, and many of the kids took better to us being grandparents. That was the case with Bruce."

Constance cleared her throat and continued. "He broke things over the years. Put holes in the walls. He got caught smoking and drinking." Constance actually laughed. "We learned to use glue. His grandpa taught him how to mend drywall. When he got caught smoking, again, his grandpa took him out back and gave him a whopper of a cigar. Made him smoke it to a nub. Bruce was so sick, I know he smoked again, but not for a really long time. Then when he'd stolen whiskey from the cabinet, and drank it with your brother, they were thirteen, his grandpa made him drink more. When he'd thrown up enough, that was that."

"My brother never mentioned that."

"Ask him someday." Constance folded her hands in her lap. "We were trained to take care of a kid like Bruce. But the truth was, he wanted to be better than where he'd come from. It's been his mission from as far back as I can remember. Not having his own biological kids ensures that he's done what he can to stop that line of violence."

Sarah's hands shook as she lifted her fork to her lips and finally took a bite of the pie. "I love him, Mrs. Griffin. I'm going to have to get over it, because I can't let him go."

"We're all here to support you, sweetheart." She covered Sarah's hand with her own. "But you start calling me grandma, or I'll turn you over my knee."

CHAPTER 33

*C*onstance cleared the table of their empty plates, and Sarah realized it had been an hour since she'd arrived. Surely, she was keeping the woman up much later than normal.

"Thank you for inviting me over. It's getting rather late. . ." she began but Constance Griffin made a tsk noise that stopped her from excusing herself.

"We have more to discuss. Would you like coffee?"

Sarah assessed how she felt. Between the margaritas with the girls, wine with Bruce, and pie with Mrs. Griffin—Grandma— she was going to explode.

"I also have tea," Constance called from the kitchen.

"Whatever you're having will be fine," she said and Constance laughed.

"Well, I was going to add whiskey to my coffee. Shall I add some to yours?"

Sarah couldn't help but chuckle. "I'll pass on the whiskey. I still need to get home."

Constance nodded and went about making coffee. "So tell me, are you going to marry my Bruce?"

Sarah eased back in her chair. "If he asked me, I would say yes.

But, I suppose we have to figure out our feelings about, well, everything that has gone on."

"Do you now?" Constance asked as she carried two mugs of coffee to the table, the bottle of whiskey tucked under her arm.

"Can I help you?" Sarah stood and moved to Constance, taking the mugs from her.

"Thank you." She gripped the whiskey and eased herself down at the table. "His grandfather and I decided to get married after knowing each other for two months. I realize things were a little different then, but you've known Bruce you're entire life."

"You're right. And that's what I have to keep reminding myself. I know him. I know the real him. Everything I've learned was about someone else."

Constance nodded. "And remember, he doesn't want to be that young boy who was brought here. He's worked very hard to be the man he is."

Sarah batted away the tears that welled in her eyes.

Constance took her hand, and gave it a squeeze. "Come with me. I want to give you something."

Sarah stood, her hands out and ready to help Constance should she need it. Instead of taking Sarah's hand, Constance laced their arms, and began to lead her down the hallway.

Pictures lined the walls, and when Constance turned on the light, Bruce smiled at Sarah at many ages. There were school photos, baseball, basketball, swim team photos, and family pictures of vacations. They didn't end at a certain age either. The most current photo of Bruce and his grandmother was from a recent Christmas.

Constance turned on the light to a bedroom and walked in, and Sarah followed.

"Bruce and his grandfather were very close. I credit him for making Bruce the man he is today. A hardworking man who loves deeply—his friends, his grandparents, and the same woman for years," she said as she winked at Sarah.

There was a warmth that resonated in Sarah's chest. Though the trauma was extensive, Bruce was gifted an amazing set of parents—grandparents.

Constance moved to a small jewelry box on her dresser that played a waltz when she opened it. From inside she pulled out a small velvet bag, and closed the lid to the box.

"I gave this to Thomas on our fifty-fifth wedding anniversary. He'd bought me a new ring on our fiftieth, and still wore the beat up band of gold we scrounged enough money for when we got married." She emptied the contents of the bag into her palm. Out fell a gold band with three diamonds. "Thomas wore this until he passed. We buried him with his original ring," she said, the hint of tears filling her voice.

"It's beautiful."

"It is," Constance said as she put it back in the bag and handed it to Sarah. "When you're ready, I want you to give this to my Bruce."

"When I'm ready?"

Constance closed her hand around Sarah's and the velvet bag. "When you're ready to get married, to commit to him, give him the ring."

Sarah swallowed hard. "You want me to propose to him?"

Constance smiled. "You kick their asses every week in a basketball game. I don't see any reason you couldn't do the asking. Besides, if you did, he'd know you trusted him and were okay with what he's done."

SARAH PULLED UP IN FRONT OF THE GUEST HOUSE. THE PORCH light was on, as well as the lamp by the window. The rest of the house was dark.

The ring that Bruce's grandmother had given her was heavy

in her pocket. Constance Griffin had said to give it to her grandson when Sarah was ready. But she wasn't ready.

Opening the center console, she set the bag inside.

THE HOUSE WAS QUIET WHEN SARAH WALKED IN, SO WHEN SHE heard movement, her heart rate spiked and her hand went to her chest.

Bruce moved from the kitchen and leaned against the doorjamb.

"You scared me," she said as she pulled off her jacket and draped it over the back of the chair.

"I didn't mean to. I'd been sitting outside enjoying the sounds of the trees. Everything else okay?" he asked.

Sarah nodded as she moved toward him. "Your grandmother is an amazing woman."

"Yes she is."

"You changed her life."

"She did the same for me," he said, reaching a hand out to her.

Sarah took his hand and eased against him.

Bruce stroked his hand over her hair. "Did she offer you insight?"

Sarah rested her head against Bruce's shoulder. "She did." Easing back, Sarah locked eyes with Bruce. "You wanted to be Bruce Griffin, which meant you did everything you could to be normal."

He smiled. "That would be true. In all honesty, minus the night in the apartment, my life has always been normal. Finding out what my father did and not wanting to carry that on, that's been my life's silent mission."

"When I pulled up in front of her house, I was flooded with memories of spending time there with you and Alex."

"Good memories I hope."

"Only the best." Sarah raised her hands to Bruce's cheeks. "I love you. I need to say thank you for trusting me with all your secrets."

"I love you. That's why you needed to know them."

"If I never have my own children, I'll always have Celia Rose and the baby."

Bruce lowered his forehead to hers. "When the time is right, we will deal with that. Like I said, there are so many options."

Sarah nodded. "After hearing your grandmother's story, I know that giving birth to a child isn't always the way to become a mother."

"And she had so much loss. The babies she lost, and the children that were sent back to parents."

"She's so proud of you. I understand that what happened to you affects every aspect of your life, but you were surrounded by good people."

Bruce ran his hand over her hair and pressed a gentle kiss to her lips. "And I still am."

CHAPTER 34

*B*ruce kissed Sarah goodbye as he headed to work. She kept her eyes closed and let exhaustion from the past few days keep her in bed until after nine o'clock, which was unheard of for her.

Her mind had continued to spin long into the early morning hours. For the first time in her life she didn't want to go for a run to clear her head, she just wanted to be still.

Eventually she couldn't be still any longer, and Sarah threw on a pair of shorts and a tank top, piled her hair on top of her head in a bun, and made a cup of coffee.

There was a cool April breeze blowing through the morning air when Sarah took her coffee to the front porch and sat in one of the rocking chairs. The grasses were still lush, butting up to the mountains. That would all change in a month when the heat rose and Colorado again became brown in color. But for those few glorious weeks, it was beautiful.

She sat surrounded by the calming song provided by Mother Nature. Birds sang, the breeze swayed the leaves on the trees, and not too far away, there was a creek that ran faster because of runoff and rain.

There had never been a day in her life she didn't appreciate the beauty that surrounded her.

As she lifted the mug, imprinted with Toby's company logo, to her lips, she heard the sound of tires on gravel. Soon the dust was visible, and then a dark SUV headed toward the house.

She didn't recognize it. Perhaps it was someone who worked for Toby, but he would have told her if someone was coming out to see her.

Doing her best to remain calm, she scanned the front porch for anything she could use if she needed to defend herself. The cup of hot coffee would only get her so far. Right near the door was a snow shovel.

The SUV came to a stop near her car. The driver turned off the car and climbed out.

The man, dressed as if he were going hiking, stepped out of the car, but stayed near the door.

"Hi," he shouted, holding up his hand.

"Hi."

"I think I took a wrong turn. I don't mean to interrupt you."

Sarah nodded slowly. "Where were you headed?"

"Flatirons Vista South."

"You're too far north," she said. "Head back out on ninety-three and turn right."

The man looked down at his phone and nodded. "Okay, I see what you're saying. I appreciate it." He lifted his head and studied her. "You look really familiar."

"I don't think so."

"I've met you." He looked away as if he were thinking of her name. "Sarah?"

There was an immediate hammering in her chest. "And you are?"

The man stepped to the front of his SUV, but stopped there. "Austin Wilkes." Sarah shook her head with no recollection of the name. "You work with Emily, correct?"

"Yes."

"I was at their wedding."

Sarah nodded slowly now. She didn't remember meeting him, but then again, maybe she'd had too much champagne, or something.

"Oh, okay. That was a good day."

"A great day," he added. "Let her know I say hello."

"I'll do that."

Austin Wilkes raised his hand in a wave again and then ducked back into his car. A moment later he backed up, rolled down the window, and waved again. "Thanks again for the directions."

She lifted her mug in salute and watched the stranger drive away.

AFTER FINISHING HER COFFEE, SARAH WENT BACK INTO THE HOUSE and showered. Her thoughts kept going back to her conversation with Bruce's grandmother, and the ring in her car.

As she wiped the condensation from the mirror, Sarah studied herself. There were dark circles under her eyes from lack of sleep. How had Bruce even gotten up and gone to work, she wondered?

There would be many more nights like that, she figured, where Bruce needed to work through things. And they wouldn't all be about his father. If things were going to work out between them, there would be fights. She liked to pick fights.

She grinned at the thought. Perhaps that was the little sister in her.

One thing was clear in her mind. She wanted to give Bruce the ring.

Sarah laughed. Never in her wildest dreams would she have thought she'd propose to a man. But more than anything, Bruce deserved it. By her asking him to marry her, it would prove that he was chosen—that she wanted him and only him.

She had his grandmother's blessing, but that wasn't enough. She needed her brother's blessing too.

Sarah pulled the towel from her hair and let it fall. Picking up her phone from the counter, she texted her brother.

What time can you get away for lunch?

She picked up her comb and ran it through her hair.

Noon, what did you have in mind?

There were the food trucks in Civic Center Park, she thought. He had talked about going there often. *Civic Center Park.*

Alex sent an emoji of a smiling face with a tongue that looked as if it were agreeing that that would be yummy. *Meet me at my office.*

Sarah set down her phone and went back to getting ready for her day, where she would ask her brother for his blessing to marry his best friend.

CHAPTER 35

The rowing machine had grown boring, so Bruce jumped on the elliptical. Toby nodded in his direction when he walked into the gym, and then climbed onto the machine next to him.

"You beat me today," Toby teased. "Did you get those reports I sent over?"

Bruce nodded. "Already approved and sent on."

"Ya know, I knew what you were capable of, but I hired you because you needed a job. The fact that you've become an invaluable asset is just a bonus. We should talk about you heading up your own team."

Bruce sped up his machine. "Will it pay better?"

Toby laughed. "Yes, but is that what you're about?"

Wiping his face with his towel, but keeping one hand on the machine, Bruce shrugged. "I'm thinking about buying a rock and half a mortgage."

Toby stopped his machine, so Bruce followed.

"You're going to ask Sarah to marry you?"

"I am." Bruce ran the towel over his head. "We've already discussed it, but I promised her an amazing proposal."

"Then we'd better get you started on that promotion today," Toby lifted his phone from the console and typed in a few notes. "Let's meet at three in my conference room."

"You don't have to give me a promotion. I'm grateful for the house and the job."

"Buddy, I can't do much for people around me but offer them what they deserve. You guys are my brothers. If someone needs a job, I can handle giving them one. But when that someone proves to me that they are management material, I'm going to put them there. You'd never let me down."

"Now I'm freaking out."

Toby laughed. "If I've learned anything in the past twenty-four hours, it's that you're the most resilient, most courageous man I know. Your desire to overcome impresses the hell out of me. This isn't a position I'd give to just anyone. It's a position I'd give to someone who would have my back and who I could trust. That's you." Toby held out his hand to Bruce.

Bruce took in a deep breath and shook Toby's hand. "You don't know what it all means to me."

"I think I do. Now, get off this stupid thing and get back on the rower. I'll race you down the Thames."

Bruce laughed. Who would have thought that the quiet multi-millionaire who liked to race virtually down rivers would be Bruce's saving grace for a third time. What could he ever possibly offer him in return?

SARAH WAITED IN THE RECEPTION AREA FOR ALEX TO COME TO HER. The lady at the front desk had paged him, and Sarah thought it made him seem pretty important.

When he appeared, Sarah stood from the chair she occupied. "Must be nice to have a staff at your beck and call."

"Doesn't suck," he said as he put his arm around his sister's shoulders and started toward the elevator. "You look tired today."

"I'm exhausted."

"Long night for you guys, huh?" he asked as he pushed the button to the elevator.

"Emotional. And after Bruce talked to me, he sent me to his grandmother's house."

The elevator door opened to a car full of people, and their conversation halted until they reached the lobby.

"He made you talk to his grandmother?" Bruce asked as they started their walk toward the park.

"I'm glad I went. I remembered that she was a really nice lady. And when I pulled up in front of the house, I had nothing but good memories of hanging out there."

"You were always underfoot."

Sarah shrugged. "Bruce let me be."

Alex nodded. "You're right. I think I'd send you home, and he'd say you could stay."

"He always had my back."

"What did his grandmother have to say?"

Brushing her hair back, Sarah collected her thoughts. "She confirmed everything that Bruce told me. She said that what made him the person he is today was his will to do so. He always wanted normality. He didn't want to be like his father."

"You're okay with who he is?"

"I am." When they'd crossed the street and headed toward the trucks, Sarah stopped. "He made it so that he'd never have kids."

Alex nodded. "What do you think about that?"

"It hurts, and that's selfish. He doesn't want to pass on those genetics."

"Do you blame him?"

"Not in the least. I just have to get over the fact that my children will never have his eyes, or his color hair."

Alex rested his hand on her shoulder. "You should talk to

Catherine about that. I think she felt the same way when I left to get Celia Rose. How could she love her knowing that she was half me and half someone else, but she'd never be any part of Catherine."

"She fell in love with her though. Fast and hard."

"She did. And Celia Rose is a lucky girl to have her as her mother. Just as Bruce was to have his grandparents."

"He said we could use a donor. I could have my own baby."

"That's something to think about."

Sarah nodded and they walked toward a fish and chips truck. They ordered and Alex paid for lunch.

They carried their lunch to a small table and sat down.

"So, the real reason I came to talk to you is because I need your blessing for something," Sarah began as Alex dipped his fish into the tartar sauce.

"My blessing?" he asked with his mouth full.

Sarah opened her purse and pulled out the velvet bag. She handed it to him, and he took it cautiously.

When he'd poured the ring into the palm of his hand, he looked up at her. "What is this?"

"His grandfather's ring."

Alex swallowed down his bite. "His grandmother gave this to you?"

"Yeah."

"Why?"

Sarah picked up a french fry and dragged it through the ketchup before biting down on it. She gave careful thought to her answer before she swallowed.

"She wants me to give it to Bruce when I'm ready to get married."

"So at your wedding?"

She shook her head. "She thinks I should propose to him. If I do that, that'll tell him that I'm okay with him. I'll mean that I accept what he's done to stop his bloodline. I'll say I trust him."

Alex slid the ring back in the bag. "So what does this have to do with me?"

"As his closest friend, I want your blessing to ask him to marry me."

Alex picked up his napkin and wiped his mouth. "I don't think you should ask me that."

"You love him."

"As much as I love you, but you know how I feel about this."

"After everything, you're still going to be an asshole and forbid me from marrying him?"

Alex's shoulders dropped. "No." He tossed down his napkin. "No, I'm not going to do that. You know everything now."

She did, more than even her brother knew.

"I would be devastated if someone told me I couldn't be with my wife. I have a beautiful daughter, and another baby on the way. A year and a half ago I was drunk and lost my job. Bruce has overcome so much more than I could ever imagine."

"So? What do you say? Give me your blessing—and mean it?"

Alex stood from the small table and held his hand out to his sister. She stood and he wrapped her in his arms. "I've always wanted the best for you and the best for Bruce. I just didn't know it would come in the same package." He kissed the top of her head. "I give you my blessing. He's lucky to have you."

CHAPTER 36

*T*he smile that had formed on Sarah's face was still intact hours later when she returned home. She was going to carefully plan out the most amazing proposal.

She'd submitted her design proposals for the new townhouse, second guessed them, then wondered if she should have asked Bruce for his input. But she'd decided against it. They could change anything after they moved in. All she wanted was to close on the property and get moved into their own home.

Maybe she could do something on their first night there. That would be a nice way to celebrate their new living arrangement.

As Sarah parked her car in front of the house her phone buzzed in her purse. She pulled it out and read the text.

I'm going to be late getting home. Wait dinner on me. I got a promotion and Toby is building me a team. I'll tell you all about it over dinner and we will celebrate. I love you.

The smile she'd been wearing now for an hour grew even wider. Toby wouldn't hand him a promotion without Bruce being worthy of it. This was a big step. She couldn't wait to celebrate with him.

Sarah gathered her things and stepped out of the car. When

her phone buzzed again, her smile continued. What more did he have to brag about?

She didn't read the ID first, she simply looked at the text.

Can you have Emily call me? She's not answering my texts or picking up my calls.

Sarah reread the message and realized it was Emily's husband who was texting her.

I'm off today. I haven't talked to her. Maybe she's in meetings.

Sarah let herself into the house and set down her things when Gordon replied.

Probably. I'll talk to her when she gets home. Have a good one!

Sarah thought about Emily and Gordon's wedding, where she'd been the maid of honor. She remembered thinking that someday she wanted what they had. They were in love, so in love, and it resonated to everyone that knew them.

Did she have that now, she wondered? Yeah, according to everyone she'd talked to, her and Bruce were no surprise to anyone—only themselves. She deserved this kind of happiness, Sarah thought. It was her turn at true love.

BRUCE SAT AT THE CONFERENCE TABLE WITH TOBY AND FOUR other people. Had Toby been planning this, he wondered as he looked around. How could he have pulled a team together so quickly.

"Okay, with the growth of T433, we need to concentrate on expansion. I want to hit our hub near headquarters, and that's what this team is for. Bruce here is going to head it up. He helped develop T433, so he has the intel. Aubrey is your human relations contact. You'll hire your own staff," he directed at Bruce. "Mike is your sales force manager. You two will work together to build a sales team. I have you budgeted for five. We'll see what they do. And Austin just relocated here from the

Chicago area, he's your IT guy. He'll help get you set up for your team."

Bruce looked at the faces of the others that had been pulled into the meeting. Had they been prepared for this transition? Was he the only one taken by surprise?

As the meeting continued, he got more involved. He'd written through one legal pad with notes, and Toby got him another. Aubrey had been with HR for five years. She knew all of the ins and outs, and she had a clear picture of the administrative team Bruce would need. They'd pool from the interior workings of the company before they looked outside.

Mike had led three different sales forces for Toby, and Bruce had no doubt he'd head up the right team to get the word out about T433. Every business in the area was going to want to utilize their software.

Austin was quiet, but his resume was impressive. Toby would have only put the best on the team, and Bruce knew it.

SARAH TOSSED A SALAD AND CUT UP FRUIT. SHE HAD NO IDEA WHAT time to expect Bruce, but they could open a bottle of wine and have a nice hearty salad for dinner. It would be ready and waiting for him.

Her phone rang, and she picked it up from the counter. It was Gordon again.

"Hey, Gordo."

"She didn't come home," he said, his voice full of panic. "Seriously, you didn't talk to Emily all day?"

Sarah's arms chilled. "No. I didn't talk to her. She hasn't called you all day?" Sarah knew that was odd.

"No. I have a call into your office, but everyone is gone. Do you have someone you can call?"

"I'll make some phone calls. She didn't have an off-site meeting or anything that she told you about, did she?"

"She didn't say anything. It was the normal goodbye this morning."

"Okay," Sarah sat down in the nearest chair. "Let me see what I can find out."

She looked at the clock. It was nearly seven. Emily would have long been home by then. As she dialed her boss, she noticed her hands shook.

"Hey, Sarah," Melanie's voice chimed. "You missed one helluva pot luck today," she continued.

"Mel, did you see Emily today?"

"No. She never came in. I assumed she got confused with your day off. I texted her, but didn't hear back. You guys are so ahead on your projects I didn't think a thing about it. Is she okay?"

Sarah felt the sting of tears. "I don't know. Gordon is looking for her. He said she'd never called or texted him all day. And she's not home yet."

"That's not her norm. If she's not working, she's on the phone with her husband."

"I think that's odd too," Sarah confirmed.

"I'll make a few calls. Let me know if you hear anything."

Sarah agreed, then scrolled through her phone to the next co-worker who might have seen Emily coming or going. But there was a tightness in her chest, and she couldn't explain why she was feeling completely nauseous.

CHAPTER 37

*B*ruce juggled the bouquet of flowers in one hand, and his commuter bag in the other. He bumped the door to the car closed with his hip and headed toward the house.

It was nearly nine o'clock. Getting things set up had taken a lot longer than he ever could have imagined, but the payoff was going to be worth it.

He'd owe Toby big for that one.

"Oh, honey, I'm home," Bruce sang the words as he walked in the house.

He could hear Sarah's voice coming from the back porch so he followed it. When he opened the door she jumped.

Her hair was knotted on the top of her head, her face was clean of makeup, but her cheeks were streaked as if she'd been crying. There was a notebook on the table and scribbles all over it.

Bruce set the flowers and his bag on the chair and waited for her to finish her phone call.

"Sweetheart, what's wrong?"

She moved from her seat and right into his arms, nearly knocking him to the ground. "Emily is missing."

He knew Emily. She and Sarah had been friends for years.

"What do you mean she's missing?"

Sarah sucked in a breath on a sob. "Gordon called this morning to see if I'd seen her. She wasn't returning his texts or calls. I said I wasn't at work. So then at seven he called again and said she'd never come home."

Bruce wrapped his arms around her tightly. "Okay, what can I do?"

She continued to sob against his chest. "I don't know. Gordon has called the police. I've been calling all of our friends. No one has heard from her."

"And they checked for her phone, right?"

"Yes. Nothing."

He brushed his hand down her hair. "We'll stay up and call people, or wait. I'll make something to eat."

She finally eased back. "I made a salad for when you got home. It's in the refrigerator next to the wine I was going to open to celebrate whatever news you had."

"We'll celebrate tomorrow. I'll make you up a plate and bring it out. What else can I get you?"

She gazed up at him. "I'm sorry."

"For worrying about your friend? Not in a million years, sweetheart. No need to be sorry ever. I'll be right back."

Bruce walked back into the house. He changed his clothes, then walked back into the kitchen to plate the salad that Sarah had made.

As he stood at the counter, he closed his eyes tight. Just let Emily be okay, he sent up the silent prayer.

Whenever someone went missing, his mind would always go back to the day he'd learned about what his father had done to those other women. Someone sat at home sobbing for them to come home too. Sadly, he hoped for an accident, and that Emily was lost in some hospital for the moment. That would be the best outcome for a worst case scenario.

SUNDAY MORNING BRUCE PULLED HIS BAG FROM THE BACK OF HIS car and walked into the YMCA. Toby shot free throws with Connor on the smaller net, and Charlotte was singing to Celia Rose.

Rachel nursed Angela, and Kelly sat next to Ray as he pulled on his shoes.

"You're light in the partner department," Alex said with a nod in Bruce's direction.

"She's not coming," he said, his voice dripping with the angst that Sarah had been feeling that morning.

Alex moved to him. "She's okay?"

"Emily is missing."

"Shit! When did this happen?"

Bruce ran his hand over the back of his neck. "Friday. She never showed for work. Early this morning they found her car."

Alex closed his eyes and Bruce knew the thoughts running through his head, and that he was sick because of them. "Man, if you need to go home. . ."

"She wants me here. She wants some alone time to process."

"She's been having to do that a lot this week."

It wasn't aimed as a jab, so Bruce talked himself down from feeling as though it were one. "We all have. She's resilient."

"More so than most people."

"Besides, my grandmother is absolutely taken by her, so it means she's good people. Like, the best of the good people."

That made Alex smile. "I couldn't agree more."

SARAH PACED THE LIVING ROOM. HER TEARS HAD RUN DRY, BUT HER insides still twisted. Where had Emily gone?

Emily was completely in love with her husband, so there was

no way she took off on her own. Her car had been found just west of Central City, of all places. What in the hell had she been doing up there?

Sarah thought about talking to her the day before. She would have said something to Sarah if she'd meant to take off. This just wasn't making any sense.

When the front door opened, Sarah jumped. She hadn't even heard Bruce drive up.

"No new news?" he asked as he set his gym bag by the door.

Sarah shook her head. "There are search parties. Search parties!" She moved to him and he held her against him.

"Do we need to go be part of them?"

"Gordon asked that I stay in town and keep in touch with everyone we work with."

Bruce ran his hand over her hair. "Okay. That's what we'll do." He kissed the top of her head. "Do you want me to call Rachel for you?"

Sarah lifted her eyes to his. "I'm okay. I'll let you know. But, what about you? God, this can't be easy for you."

"I'm okay too. I'm just worried about you. This isn't easy."

"She wouldn't have just run away."

He pulled her to him again. "They'll find her."

When her tears had dried again, Sarah wiped her eyes. "You never did tell me about your promotion."

Bruce ran his hands down her back. "It's not so important."

"I need some good news."

"Toby gave me a promotion. He said I was invaluable to his company, and not just because I was his friend. I have a team management in place, and we'll start building our own team to move out the product I've been working on since I got there."

Sarah blinked hard and smiled. "That's fantastic."

"It is."

"I might have a few late nights, but it'll be worth it."

Sarah looped her arms around his neck and pressed a gentle kiss to his lips. "I'm proud of you."

"Thank you." He held her a moment longer. "I need to get a shower. Would you like to join me?"

She let out a sigh. "I think I would. I need something to occupy my mind for a bit."

CHAPTER 38

*S*arah sat at her desk clicking the pen in her hand. Her focus was gone. It had been a week, and Emily hadn't returned to her desk, or her home.

The email on Sarah's computer screen had the closing details for her townhouse, but knowing something had happened to her dear friend took the joy out of everything. Even Bruce's grandfather's ring still sat in the center console of her car without another thought for now.

Sickness swirled in her. She needed to get out, take a walk, process her feelings.

I'm home early, the text came across her phone and she picked it up. *Grandma had a doctor appointment. I'll make us a nice dinner and we'll lock ourselves in the house all weekend. I love you.*

Sarah touched the screen as if it brought Bruce closer to her in that moment. He was her rock, and she hoped she was enough of one for him too.

~

BRUCE UNLOADED THE GROCERIES FOR THE WEEKEND, LEAVING OUT the steaks he'd planned to cook for the night. He'd already told the guys that he and Sarah would skip basketball on Sunday. Until Emily was found, he figured Sarah was going to need some time.

After he'd taken his grandmother to her doctor appointment, he'd had a phone call with his therapist. Keeping calm through everything happening to Sarah was taking its toll on him, and he knew why. He needed to face it head on and be strong for her.

This personally didn't have anything to do with him, his father, or the blood that pumped through his veins. And, he'd checked to make sure his father was right where he was supposed to be.

Bruce still prayed that Emily was in some hospital trying to figure out who she was because she'd hit her head and had amnesia, but they didn't have a trail, so his prayers were going unanswered.

He looked up when he heard the tires on the gravel. Taking two bottles of water from the refrigerator, he opened them and walked to the door.

Sarah sat in her car, her head back against the headrest and her eyes closed. He knew this method of calming before going into the house. Giving her a moment, he waited by the door until he heard her open the car door and step out.

"You got off early too?" he asked as he walked toward her.

"I can't focus. I can't get any work done."

Bruce stepped to her, handing her a bottle, and kissing her gently. "We're just going to have a peaceful weekend, you and me. No internet. No emails. No need to leave the house because I got groceries."

Sarah leaned against him. "Thank you."

"Let's go inside. I was getting everything put away so I could start dinner. Why don't you go take a nice warm shower?"

"I think I will."

They walked through the front door and he knew Sarah had seen the new bouquet of flowers he'd picked up and put in a vase on the coffee table.

"Those are lovely," she said.

"It's important to bring nice things into the house," he offered. "It reminds us there is still beauty in the world."

She nodded slowly. "There hasn't been one clue. Not one."

"I don't have any words, Sarah. They won't forget her. They'll keep looking."

"I know. I just want her home." She dropped her bag by the door and walked to the bedroom, shutting the door behind her.

BRUCE SAT IN HIS OFFICE ON MONDAY MORNING WITH HIS COFFEE mug in hand. He was going to need an entire pot of coffee just to get through the first few hours.

The weekend had been a restless one for Sarah, and the longer it went without word from Emily, the more stirred up she became.

Bruce would always be there for her, no matter what the outcome was, but it was starting to rattle him.

When Emily had first disappeared, he assumed there just was something wrong at home. Though Sarah assured him that she was happily married and in love with her husband, it seemed logical. When they found her car, then he began to worry.

In the office there had been discussion on the serial killer documentary, and though he never reacted to any of it, he'd heard more than he'd have liked to.

His own father had taken women, in their cars, and they would then find them abandoned. There had been no rhyme or reason to where they'd found the cars, but he'd buried all of their bodies in the same place.

When his stomach lurched at the thought, Bruce had to force

himself to keep his coffee down. This was a random situation. This had nothing to do with him. He wasn't his father, he reminded himself.

There was a knock on his office door and Austin pushed open the door slightly.

"Do you have a minute?"

Bruce wiped the back of his hand over his brow, set down his coffee, and nodded.

Austin walked toward his desk. "I need to head to Florida for a few days. I just got some family news. I can still check in, but I wanted..."

Bruce held up his hand. "Family is really important. If it's only a few days, we can manage."

Austin smiled. "Thanks. I knew you'd understand. I hear about how you talk about your grandmother and your girlfriend. They're important to you."

Bruce couldn't recall mentioning either of them, though they were important. Perhaps he did bring them up in casual conversation. "Yeah. They're fantastic facets in my life."

"I'll check in. I'm caught up on the reports and all."

"Go. We've got it."

Austin thanked him one more time before walking out of the office and closing the door behind him.

Bruce scrubbed his hands over his face. What would he do without his grandmother and Sarah? If he was a lucky man, he'd never have to know.

CHAPTER 39

"*H*er phone pinged!" Sarah yelled into the phone just beyond her office building on the path she walked during lunch. "Someone turned it on."

"Okay, so this is good, right?" Bruce asked.

"I don't know," the tears had broken through the moment of excitement, and Sarah sat on the bench. "It means someone has her things. So maybe they have her."

"Did Gordon call you?"

"Yes. He's on his way to Florida where the signal is coming from."

"Florida?"

"Maybe she did run away. Maybe after three weeks she's come to her senses. I'll accept that. Maybe she wasn't as happy as I thought."

"Keep me posted. Call Rachel too. Just walk through it with her. Trust me. It'll do a lot of good."

Sarah let out a breath. "Okay. I'll do that. I love you."

"I love you too," he said before he disconnected the call.

Sarah sat on the bench for a few more moments before heading back to her office, and past Emily's vacant desk where the photo of her and Gordon looked up at Sarah as she walked by.

They'd find her. It was all going to be okay, she promised herself.

FOR THE PAST WEEK BRUCE HAD TRIED TO BURY HIMSELF IN HIS work to keep himself sane. Austin having been gone for personal reasons, and Aubrey catching a cold hadn't helped their momentum in getting their team ready. But it had kept him busy, and that was what he'd needed.

"Where were we?" Bruce asked the group of people who had gone silent during his phone call.

"Everything okay?" Toby asked.

"I'll let you know."

Aubrey tapped her pencil to her pad. "Was your girlfriend friends with that missing woman?" Bruce shifted his glance her way. "Sorry, hard not to overhear."

Bruce nodded. "Yeah. They just got a ping to her phone in Florida."

Aubrey chewed on her lip. "They found her body in Florida," she said.

Bruce felt the air grow heavy in his lungs as Toby leaned in toward Aubrey. "They found her?"

"Yes. It was just on the news. Her phone was near her body and that's how they identified her. It came through my feed," she said as she scrolled through her phone. "The body of a Colorado woman, Emily Watkins, missing nearly three weeks was found just outside of Pensacola, Florida where another woman, Mindy Martin-Jones was abducted last week in a parking lot—"

Bruce felt the blood drain from his face and Toby stood to ease him into his chair.

Mike stood and filled a glass with water from the dispenser, handing it to Toby who pressed it into Bruce's hand. "Drink."

Bruce blinked and sipped.

Mike closed his binder with the sales figures. "Who is Mindy Martin-Jones?"

Toby surveyed the room. The small team they'd put in place a had grown to ten people who all watched their manager take a blow. Bruce tried to get out of his head. It was coincidence. It was a common name. Damnit! Mindy Martin.

"Why don't we gather back later? I'll send you all an email," Toby said.

The team began to gather their items.

Austin stood and tucked his notebook into his commuter bag. "Is there anything I can do?"

Toby shook his head. "He'll be fine."

Austin nodded and let himself out of the office.

When they were all gone, Toby pulled up a chair next to Bruce and sat down. "Coincidence, right?"

"Not unless my life took a turn. Sarah's best friend. My ex-girlfriend?"

"Too tidy?"

"Not done," Bruce said sucking in a breath. "I let you all know about my family, and now this."

Toby ran his tongue over his teeth. "I'm going to let that slide. You don't mean to accuse your best friends—your brothers—in this, right?"

Bruce scrubbed his hands over his face. "No. With that fricking documentary out there, someone is bound to get ideas."

"And you think that's what's happening?"

Bruce shrugged. "I don't know. I've never known anyone who disappeared before, have you?"

Toby shook his head.

"And now Emily disappears and they find her phone where a Mindy Martin-Jones was taken? Mindy moved to Florida when we broke up. She got married. She has kids."

"You think someone is personally gunning for you?"

"Or idolizing my father," he sad and his stomach clenched. "When they put that shit on TV and glamorize it, it feeds those who need it."

"Can you stop it from airing?"

"What's to stop? Even Sarah watched the damn thing." Bruce leaned back in his chair. "I have to find out if it was the same Mindy. I also need to get to Sarah. If I know about Emily, it'll only be a moment before she does."

BRUCE WAS RIGHT. AS HE DROVE HOME, HE RECEIVED SARAH'S hysterical phone call. It was all he could do to get her to pull over on the side of the road until he could reach her. When he did, she flew from her car and straight into his arms, and sobbed on the side of the highway.

"He killed her!" she screamed. "He killed her!"

Bruce ran his hand over her hair. "I know," he said softly. "I know."

"Son-of-a-bitch!"

There were no words. How was he supposed to console the woman he loved when he was damn sure it was personal?

"Let's get home. Can you drive? I'll follow you."

Sarah sucked in a breath, and then another. "I'm scared."

Bruce pulled her to him again. "I know, sweetheart. I'm not going to let anything ever happen to you." And that promise was one he intended to keep.

Until she could drive, he'd hold her on the side of the highway that butted up to the majestic Rocky Mountains. No matter how grandly they rose around them, nothing was bigger than the feelings Sarah was working through.

Of course, Bruce battled inside himself. He was going to need to dig into his father's history. Was this someone who had gone through similar pain when his father took a loved one? Was this someone who watched that damned documentary and thought it would be thrilling? Was it random, and he only felt the spotlight on himself?

He didn't know. But he closed his eyes tightly and sent a prayer out for Mindy's safe return. No child should have to lose their mother like that.

CHAPTER 40

*I*t had taken the better part of two hours, but Bruce was able to convince Sarah to lay down. He stood in the kitchen swallowing down Tylenol for his pounding head when Rachel walked in the door.

"Where is she?" she asked setting her purse on the couch.

"I just made her lay down. She's extremely worked up."

"Of course she is," Rachel moved to him and rested her hand on his arm. "And how are you? This hits a little close to home, doesn't it?" Her brows rose to emphasize her point.

Bruce looked toward the bedroom, as if to check that the door was shut so he could talk freely.

"Mindy Martin went missing."

"Your ex-girlfriend?"

Bruce nodded and leaned against the counter again. "Emily's body was found in the area where Mindy went missing."

Rachel rubbed her fingers over her brow. "Now it really hits home."

"I think someone is either targeting people I know, or because of that damn documentary, they're doing some idolizing."

"We need to tell someone—call the cops."

"I've thought about that. I just don't want to invite more drama into my life if that's not what's happening. I need to dive into my father's case. I know some things. But I know very few specifics, on purpose."

"Maybe your friends should do that for you then. And maybe we should call in the tip, anonymously at least?"

He shook his head. "Maybe I should go see him—my dad."

Rachel's eyes went wide. "I think that's a bad idea."

"I think we need to stop this person before they get to one of you."

She worried her lip as she kept her gaze on him. "And I think we should leave that to the professionals."

SARAH TAPPED HER FINGERS ON THE TABLE AT THE TITLE COMPANY. She'd left work early to close on her house.

She sat at the table with closing documents to her new house in a tidy folder. She'd spent the better part of an hour signing documents that were all going to be scanned and emailed anyway. What a waste of papers, she thought to herself as she clicked the pen over and over.

She hadn't been ready to leave the room. Her new keys were heavy in her hand.

How could she go forward with her life, her new and shiny life, when Emily was dead?

And, Sarah had heard the news. That woman in Florida was Mindy Martin.

Sarah's hands shook so she laid them flat on the table.

There was doubt in her head, and it was creeping into her heart. Bruce knew both of the women. The only thing that kept her sane was that he'd been near her the entire time—and she loved him so much, she couldn't believe he'd do such a thing.

Then doubt snuck back in. Could he have masterminded it?

She shook the thought away. No. Bruce had gone to extremes to not be like his father. He wasn't going to take that path.

"Is everything okay?" one of the women who worked at the title company poked her head into the office.

"Yes. I'm sorry. I think I'm just trying to wrap my head around finally closing on the house."

"We get that a lot. Can I get you a bottle of water or a soda? You look a little pale. And we get that a lot, too."

Finally, there was some lightness in Sarah's chest. "I'll be fine. Thank you."

The woman gave her a polite nod, and walked away.

THERE WAS NEW CAR SMELL, AND THEN THERE WAS NEW FUTURE smell, Sarah thought as she pushed open the front door to her new house.

Contractor white walls, the echo of her footsteps, and the thought of how much she had wanted that space. Only now as she looked around, she realized just how homey the guest house was. Could she make this sterile space homey too?

With Bruce she could.

She walked in further and took a moment to sit down on the newly carpeted stairs. In her moment of doubt, she still wanted that home with Bruce. That was a positive sign, wasn't it? Her mind still focused on the happiness she had with him?

Tears stung her eyes. It was all coincidence, right? Yes, there was no reason to think otherwise.

Congratulations! The text popped up on her phone from a number she didn't recognize. *It's a nice place.*

Sarah studied the phone number, but it wasn't familiar. *Thank you*, she replied. *Who is this?*

Before there was a reply, she heard a cell phone ringing. Her heart began to hammer in her chest as she stood and cautiously walked through the house to the kitchen. The ringing grew louder.

She followed the noise to the pantry, and when she opened the door, there was a cell phone ringing on the shelf.

Sarah let out a nervous laugh as she picked up the phone, and realized it was familiar. The pink sparkly case was Rachel's.

Holding the phone with both hands, because they'd begun to tremble, she slid her finger over the screen, and unlocked the phone.

"Emily was one. Mindy is two. Rachel will be three. Only five more to go," the voice said on the other end of the phone.

Sarah stopped breathing as the line went dead. No. No. No.

"What are you doing?" Bruce's voice came from behind her. Both her phone and Rachel's dropped from her hands and crashed to the floor as she screamed.

Fear took over, and survival mode kicked in as she rushed him, slamming him backward against the wall.

"Don't you hurt her, you son-of-a-bitch!" she screamed at him as she beat her hands against him.

"What are you talking about?" Bruce grabbed her wrists.

"Rachel. Where is she?" she screamed, not even recognizing her own voice.

"I don't know. I just came from my office. Sarah, what is going on? You're scaring the hell out of me."

"You killed Emily and Mindy!"

The expression that shifted on his face burned into her core. She hadn't meant to say that. She didn't believe it, did she?

Bruce let go of her wrists and walked toward the front door.

No, he hadn't killed them. But the flash in his eyes said Sarah's accusation had stabbed him right in the heart.

CHAPTER 41

*T*he blood rushing in his ears was deafening. There was a throbbing behind his eyes, and his skin had grown hot.

Not sure if he was making it up or not, he was sure he could hear Sarah screaming for him—not at him.

But Bruce climbed into his car, started the engine, and peeled out of the driveway and away from the community that was still being erected.

There was a lot to think about, and no time. He was trying to piece everything that Sarah had screamed at him into one thought.

Where is Rachel? That phrase played over and over in his throbbing head. Hadn't Sarah had Rachel's phone in her hand?

Bruce picked up his phone and pressed the contact photo for Craig, as he sped down the highway toward town.

"Man, I just got the baby down," Craig's voice wearily sighed into the phone.

"Where's your wife?"

"Out."

"Seriously! Tell me where the hell she is."

"What the fu—"

"Something is going on. I don't want to scare you, but I think she's in danger. I need to know where the hell she is." Bruce crossed the double yellow line to pass the car in front of him, darting back just in time.

"She's with Catherine."

"Call Catherine and make sure she's with her. Call her now. Check on her. Get her on the damn phone."

"Okay. Okay, hold on," Craig agreed as he put Bruce on hold.

Bruce continued his speed down the highway waiting for Craig to get back to him.

"I got her," Craig's voice rang back in his ear. "She lost her phone."

"It was lifted from her."

"Seriously, Bruce—"

"Just get her home. If Alex isn't home, take Catherine and Celia Rose too. We need to get everyone in one place."

There was a moment of silence. "I heard about Mindy. Dude, I'm sorry."

"They haven't found her yet, and it's a little too cozy, don't you think."

"You think this is personal?"

"I think someone is sending a message directly to me." Then he realized he'd run out on Sarah. "Shit! I gotta go. Get them to your house, now!"

Bruce found an opening in traffic and flipped to go the other way. Again, he crossed double yellows to get around those not going quite his pace.

He called Toby. "Get to my grandmother's house," he said immediately.

"I'm in a meeting. What's going on?"

"I don't really know. I just think the women in my life are in danger. You need to get to my grandmother."

"Okay. I'll be there."

He made the same phone call to Ray before he noticed the sirens and lights coming up behind him. He was at the entrance to the neighborhood, and if he just kept going, he could be pulled up in front of Sarah's new townhouse in less than a minute. How could he have run out on her?

Because she'd accused him of murder, that's how.

With the police car right on his tail, Bruce pulled over.

As soon as he put his car in park, he opened the door, unbuckled his seatbelt, and climbed out. His mind was racing a million miles a minute, and he didn't have time for a ticket. What he needed was the officers' help. He was afraid that there were lives in danger, and this was a waste of time.

The officer stood behind his car door, his hand on the butt of his gun.

"Sir, do not move," he said, shouting over the traffic that passed them. "Please put your hands on the car."

"Listen, I need your help," Bruce called back to him.

"I need you not to move. Do you have any weapons?" the officer asked as another officer pulled up.

"No. But I think my girlfriend might be in some trouble."

"Who is your girlfriend?" the officer shouted as four more police cars flew down the highway with their sirens and lights.

Bruce watched as they turned into the neighborhood.

His knees went weak as he gripped the side of his car. "Sarah Burke. She's in that neighborhood. I don't remember the exact address, but it's programmed into my phone."

The officers moved slowly toward him, one on each side of the car, and each with their hands on the butts of their guns.

"I'm going to ask you to move to the rear of your car and sit on the ground." Bruce complied.

One officer stood guard as the other moved toward his open door.

"Where is your phone?"

"In the cup holder. You have my permission to take it out and look at it. We need to get to my girlfriend."

The officer cautiously took Bruce's phone out of the car. Bruce gave him the code to access it.

The officer scrolled through the texts and contacts, looking toward the other officer.

Then Bruce heard the chime as another text message came through.

He watched the officer's eyes go wide.

"Brett Bennett, I know who you are, and you owe me this one," the officer read the text. "Is this your girlfriend?"

The officer turned the phone toward Bruce and showed him the picture of Sarah.

Bruce swallowed hard and tears began to stream down his cheeks without warning.

"Yes. We have to get to her."

"And you're Brett Bennett?"

Bruce wiped at his eyes, making sure to keep his hands visible and open. "I am—I was. Listen, you can arrest me, I don't care. But you have to find Sarah. I think she's in danger."

"What do you mean you were Brett Bennett?"

Bruce squeezed his eyes shut tightly, then opened them to look up at the officer.

"I am the son of Sam Bennett."

Again, the officers exchanged glances. "Serial killer?"

"Yes."

"And now you go by another name?"

"I am legally Bruce Griffin, and I have been since I was eleven. But I think someone is trying to copycat my father's destruction, or is making me pay for it."

"Why do you say that?"

This was taking too damn long, but he knew he'd be shot right here if he didn't just keep talking.

"A friend of my girlfriend was kidnapped and killed. Whoever did it left her body in the same town that my ex-girlfriend went missing."

"What are their names?"

Bruce sucked in a breath. "Emily Watkins was kidnapped between her home and work, here in Boulder. Mindy Martin-Jones went missing in Florida, where they found Emily's body."

The officer behind him moved toward him.

"What was your girlfriend's name again?"

"Sarah Burke."

Bruce cranked his neck to look up at the officer who once again exchanged stern looks with the other officer.

"They responded to a 9-1-1 call from a Sarah Burke about ten minutes ago. She said there was an intruder in her house, but the call was dropped."

Bruce thought of her screaming at him and his head began to spin. Had someone been in the house at that moment or had she called the police on him?

The image of the police cars that had passed them with their lights and sirens replayed in his mind. They were responding to her.

"Did they find her?" Bruce asked. "Please find out if they have her."

The officer shook his head. "The house was empty except for two different cell phones."

CHAPTER 42

The zip ties around Sarah's wrists dug into her skin as she fought them. She'd been thrown into the car, head first, and now she struggled to even breathe on the floor, pinned between the front and back seat.

The man who drove cackled as the car picked up speed.

"That's right. Arrest that man for all of this. That would be epic," he said aloud. "Looks like your lover boy has been apprehended."

Sarah assumed they were on the highway just outside the neighborhood. What did he mean they'd apprehended her lover boy? The police had Bruce?

Tears stung her eyes and blood dripped from her nose where she'd hit the floor of the car with her face.

"I've waited twenty years for this moment. Twenty years!" he yelled from the front. "I'll get all of you. I'll leave you scattered just like he did."

Sarah managed to wiggle enough to be on her side. She sucked in a deep breath.

The man had come out of nowhere in the empty house. She'd been blindsided and knocked back against the wall. His fist had gone into her stomach, his elbow into her cheek, and his knee into her groin. When she'd gone down, he'd tied those zip ties around her hands and dragged her through the kitchen and out to the garage where his car had been parked.

He'd been in the house, she realized in that moment. He'd been in her nice, contractor white, clean house!

It stirred in her belly, along with the sickening motion from the car. He'd kill her if she threw up on the floor, so she swallowed it down and prayed for strength.

As the car weaved from side to side, Sarah tried to remember every detail.

She hadn't seen him coming at her. Was he tall? Was he fit? Did he have hair?

It was a blur. It had happened so quickly.

Okay, she didn't know who he was, so she tried to pay attention to the road. Before he'd picked up speed, the car had certainly taken a left. They were headed south.

Now that she could see out the window, slightly, and only the sky, she watched for markers she might know. Trees, or posts. Maybe they'd pass under a street sign.

The road eventually turned to gravel. She could hear it under the tires.

How far out on the gravel had they gone? She wasn't sure, but the hard turn and hill was familiar. He was taking her home. He was taking her to the guest house.

Bruce, he would be there.

It wasn't Bruce that had attacked her. She would have known if it was. This man was shorter, much shorter.

Now the tears were hot on her cheeks.

She'd accused Bruce. What had she done? He'd walked out on her.

Rachel! Oh, God! The caller said something about Rachel.

She almost couldn't fight off the sickness now.

When the car lurched to a stop, Sarah rolled into the front seats, again, hitting her face.

A moment later the back door was opened and she was yanked out by her feet. Her back scraped against the metal until she was dropped on the ground, her head bouncing back against the car.

"You look like shit," the man growled and raised his sunglasses.

She had to focus. This was the first time she was seeing his face. And she knew his face.

"You're going to get up and walk. You're too freaking tall for me to be dragging you over the ground," he demanded as he grabbed her by the shirt and yanked her up as she tried to stabilize her feet under her. "If you yell, I'll kill you. If you run, I'll shoot you. If you fight, I'll stab you," he said pulling a long-bladed knife from the sheath on his side.

She studied his face. Where had she seen this man?

He pushed her so that she would walk, and he held the tip of the knife to her back.

They weren't far from the guest house, Sarah recognized the surroundings.

"Why did you bring me here?" she asked and felt the tip of the knife dig into her skin.

"You want to ask questions? Lovely," the man growled. He didn't answer, but kept guiding her toward the trees with the tip of the knife in her back. "Head to that shed."

Sarah had once come across the utility shed on a hike. They were about a mile behind the guest house and two from the highway.

"Why are you doing this?" she asked, knowing the pain of the knife would be greater, but she had to keep him talking.

She was right. The knife went through her shirt now, and she could feel the trickle of blood roll down her back.

"He killed my mother. He robbed me of my mother. You don't

just get to do that and then rot in jail where they provide you with a life."

Sarah swallowed hard. "Who killed your mother?"

This time he shoved her and she landed on the ground, again taking the brunt of the fall right to her face as her hands had gone numb tied behind her.

The man put his boot on her shoulder and rolled her to her back, where her arms pinched under her. It was then she got her first true look at him.

He might have been her age. Not even thirty. He had a professional haircut, and even his clothes appeared to be something he'd wear to a job in an office. This man didn't look like some deranged backwoods killer.

And then it hit her. This was the man who had come up on her at the guest house. The man who had taken the wrong turn looking for the hiking trail. For the life of her she couldn't remember his name, but she knew him.

God! He'd been scoping her out. She'd talked to the man that killed Emily, and she'd never thought another thing about it.

"Now get the hell back up and walk. Stop asking so many damn questions. You're not going to get out of this alive anyway, so you don't need to know shit!"

CHAPTER 43

They had nothing to arrest Bruce for, but the ticket they'd had to issue him was hefty. The saving grace of it all, was that he convinced them to follow him to Toby's guest house so he could check for Sarah, and then give them a report as to what he knew.

Sarah hadn't been home, and Bruce made a clean sweep of the house and the yard before he sat down with the officers at the table.

"My father would abduct his victims in public places. Twenty years ago, there were fewer cameras to catch his activity, and not very many cell phones. But he'd take one victim, and keep her." He had to swallow down the lump that had formed in his throat. "When she was too weak, he'd kill her, and dump her body nearby, and take another victim."

His skin was clammy and his mouth had gone dry. When Sarah came back to him, he'd never speak of his father again. He swore it.

"Did your father stay in one area ?" the officer asked, and Bruce heard more cars out front.

"It all happened within a ten mile radius of where we lived."

"But this guy already has gone across the country. Why do you think he's mimicking your father's path?"

Bruce shrugged. "He called me by my birth name. I think he's using people close to me for revenge."

The officers exchanged glances. "Perhaps a kid who lost a mother?"

"That's what I'm thinking," Bruce said as he rose and opened the refrigerator to pull out a bottle of juice.

"We'll put a call through to the department in Florida."

Bruce nodded in agreement. "Can I offer you something to drink?"

The men shook their head as the front door flew open and Alex pushed past the officers and straight for Bruce, his hands coming to his chest and gripping his shirt.

"Son-of-a-bitch! Where is she? This is why I said she was forbidden. What the hell did you do to my sister?" His voice was at a pitch Bruce had never heard, and his eyes were wild and dark.

The two officers moved in swiftly, pulling Alex from him. With hands on Alex's shoulders, they pushed him away from Bruce, both poised to take either of them down if they needed to.

"Who are you?" one of the officers asked.

"I'm Sarah Burke's goddamned brother," he spat out the words, his eyes still locked on Bruce. "I'll kill you if you hurt her," he said and Bruce wouldn't blame him if he felt the need to do just that.

"You really think I would hurt her? I'm damn sure you know better."

The officers eyed them both. "You know each other then?" the officer asked.

Alex nodded, easing himself against the officer still holding him. "Shit, yeah. This asshole is as close to a brother as I have. We've been best friends since we were eleven."

The officer eased his grip. "You haven't heard from your sister then?"

"She called and said she got her new place and I should come see it. I was on my way there when my wife called in a panic because this asshat said that something was going on." Alex ran his hands over his hair. "When I got to my sister's new place it was swarming with police."

"Where is your wife now?" the other officer asked.

"She's with her best friend Rachel, who I guess had her phone stolen. They're all safe."

Bruce lifted his chin. "Where is everyone?"

"They're all at Ray and Kelly's. And I mean everyone, including your grandmother."

That was when the front door opened again and Toby hurried into the house. "Austin Wilkes," he spat out the name.

"I don't have time for my job right now," Bruce growled, hearing the name of his IT manager.

"No, you shit," Toby continued. "Your grandmother told me that Austin Wilkes had come by her house a few times under the guise that he was selling siding. He drives a shitty Subaru, silver, with a dent in the back fender."

Bruce moved toward him. "Damnit!"

"I left her with Ray and Craig." He gripped Bruce's shoulders. "If that's true, he's planted himself in our circle."

Bruce felt his knees grow week. "He took off time last week to go to Florida."

The officer moved to the officer who had taken up guard at the door and relayed the name to him.

"Get your laptop," Toby instructed and Bruce did so, setting it up on the table as Toby began searching.

He did a basic search for Austin Wilkes and hit pay dirt.

"Catrina Wilkes, twenty-eight, was the fourth victim of the Chicago River Killer, Sam Bennett," he read the article. "Catrina was a single mother. Son Austin Wilkes, age eight—" He stopped reading.

Bruce pressed his fingers to his eyes. This was the fear he lived with his entire life. Sure, another victim of his father's would do enough research to know who Brett Bennett was.

Toby looked up at the officer, and the other five that walked into the kitchen. "I have this entire compound under video surveillance, as well as my business headquarters. I can easily have security find out when Wilkes has come and gone from the building. I can also find out if he's been on my property."

And from there, they began their investigation and search for Sarah and Mindy.

Officers were sent to Ray's house to protect the other women in Bruce's life. There would be no reason to continue on if something happened to Sarah, his grandmother, or the wives of his friends—for that matter, Mindy too. Then again, he'd never stooped as low as thinking about ending it—he wasn't going to start now.

It made sense that they'd find Mindy nearby, and he hoped that they'd find her alive. If Austin Wilkes was following in his father's footsteps, he'd have kept Mindy alive until he had Sarah. Maybe there was some hope that she was still alive.

Bruce lowered himself into a chair and tipped his head back. He'd been working with the man behind all of this for weeks. How clever he had to be, to plant himself where he had. Of course, a man with a plan could take his time. It sickened him. But, Austin Wilkes had been horribly sloppy. They had a lot of information in a short amount of time.

Was he trying to get caught?

CHAPTER 44

The shed was damp, dark, and musty. There was the distinct scent of urine and maybe blood, but she couldn't deny that that might be her. Sarah sat in the corner, her bottom wet from the ground.

The man had thrown her inside the shed and locked the door, but she wasn't sure she was alone. When she heard his car drive away, Sarah kicked her feet beneath herself and pushed up against the wall until she could stand.

God, hadn't she spent hours watching videos on the internet that said what to do if you were ever kidnapped? How come she didn't remember any of it now?

Splinters from the wall of the shed impaled her back as she slid against it and rose. The ties dug into her wrists and the need to free her arms led to the contemplation of how to attempt that feat. Crouching down and stepping over her hands was the only option, but the ties were tight.

There was a good chance if she managed to step through her arms, it would dislocate her shoulder. It would hurt like a son-of-a-bitch, but it could be fixed. It wouldn't be the first time she'd have put her shoulder back in place. Layups in a championship game didn't always land a player on their feet. Sometimes the defense got in the way, and a hardwood floor was as unforgiving as the wood slats of an old shed.

Standing, Sarah walked the wall of the tiny shed to get a feel for it. As expected, there were a few items that someone might use if they were going to go out on the creek that ran beyond the property. It wasn't even big enough to be considered a river, but she supposed with enough snow runoff, it could take a kayak quite a ways.

Then she realized that was exactly what all of the items in the shed were. She bumped into three kayaks hanging on wall. Paddles were stacked on arms that hit her in the head as she turned. Keeping as close to the wall as she could, she shuffled her feet until she kicked something, and she was sure that whatever she'd kicked, whimpered.

Sarah froze. She was right. There was someone else in there.

"Hello? Is there someone else here?" she asked. The noise happened again.

Sarah closed her eyes, as if it gave her encouragement, then lowered herself to the lump beneath her.

Turning so that she could use her hands to feel, though they had mostly gone numb, she touched the pile she'd kicked. That was when the smell had hit her. If this was a person, they'd been there for days, or more.

Her back turned to the wall, she ran her hands over cloth and then felt cold, clammy skin. They moved under her fingers, and she felt a hand. The fingers were ice cold, and whoever now rested their hand in hers shook.

"I can't see in here, but maybe we can get you something to cover you up. You're freezing."

The person moaned again, as if in protest.

Sarah had a mission now. She would get them out of that shed.

~

ALEX AND BRUCE SAT AT THE TABLE WITH TOBY AS HE CLICKED away at the laptop. Officers came and went, and Bruce could hear them whisper and then respond on their radios.

He knew that there were officers with his grandmother and the rest of their friends. Mindy's family had been alerted that they had some leads, but nothing solid.

Bruce felt helpless sitting at the table, but Toby was about to give them some answers.

"Why did he go to Florida?" Toby asked and an officer moved in closer.

"He said there was a family emergency or something. I didn't pay a lot of attention. We were ahead on the project and, hell, if someone says they need to be with their family, I'm going to let them go."

Toby nodded. "I pulled up HR records of his request for time off. So I know for sure he was in the building that day. I ran through the badge scans for that day. He logged in at nine-thirty. An hour and a half late. He logged out at four."

"What does that prove?"

"Just that he was there." He pulled up the HR records, and brought Austin Wilkes' picture on the screen. "Where do I send this so you all know who you're looking for. This is a very recent photo. I can pull more from camera footage too."

The officer gave him an email address. They would begin to send out the pictures of Austin Wilkes and Sarah, as well as Mindy's photo, too.

Toby continued clicking through screens on the laptop. "Here is a current photo of the car he drove in and out in," he said and sent that photo in as well.

Watching Toby work made Bruce proud to work for him. He knew his stuff, and wasn't that part of what had made him the wealthiest S.O.B. that Bruce knew?

Toby changed screens. Zooming in with the camera, Bruce realized he was looking at camera angles from in front of his house. Bruce recognized his car, Toby's car, the housekeeper's car, and Sarah's. Then, a wave of sickness moved through him when he saw the Subaru with the dented back end drive in front of Toby's house and keep going.

"He's been out here," Toby said and the officers moved in around him.

He switched camera angles again, and this time Bruce saw the guest house.

"When was this footage?" he asked noticing Sarah's car parked there, but his was gone.

"The same morning Emily went missing. This was at seven-forty-five," Toby said. "He was here before he showed up at work."

Bruce's entire body shook as he watched the footage of Sarah walking out and talking to the man.

CHAPTER 45

*T*he temperature in the shed had dropped. Sarah's body shook as she walked the walls again.

Her hands were numb, so she used the back of her arms to feel her way around. When she got to the door, she searched for a handle.

There was a latch, and though it moved, the door was obviously locked from the outside. But the latch was at the right height that she could hook the ties around it and try to pry them free.

The ties dug deeper into her wrists, but she had to try to twist them until they gave. Taking deep breaths, Sarah twisted herself, her shoulders burning in pain. When it was excruciating, and she couldn't twist any further, she thought of Bruce, and what he must be going through after he left. Did he know yet that she was missing? Was he in danger? God, he had to be, she thought as she gave one more twist against the metal latch—and the tie loosened.

Wanting to scream out, she gritted her teeth and twisted again.

The tie gave some more. Sarah lifted it from the latch and

tried to breathe enough to calm herself, hoping that that would travel to the tips of her numb fingers and allow her hands to slip through—and they did.

She swallowed the sob of gratefulness, leaning against the door, she rubbed her hands together trying to get the feeling back.

When she could wiggle her fingers, and feel them, she moved back around the wall toward the person in the corner. When her foot kicked them, she knelt down again.

"My hands are free," she said, the tremble in her voice with a hint of joy.

Reaching her hands out she felt for the body against the wall. The hair was long, and matted. When her hands came across the face, it was certainly female. Sarah felt for breath, and there was the slight hint of it.

"We're going to get out of here. I swear we will. I want you to be strong," she said, not even sure if the woman could hear her. "We're not far from where I live with my boyfriend. He'll find us. He's so smart," she said and the tears were back. "He knows what's going on. I know he does."

Sarah eased back up. The paddles on the wall could help her get them out of there. Maybe there was a loose board on the walls, or maybe the door could be opened.

If that failed, he'd be back, but she'd be ready for him. Sarah Burke could kick any man's ass, when he didn't blindside her.

She gritted her teeth. That alone was worth the ass kicking she was going to give him.

THE NUMBER OF OFFICERS AND CARS HAD DOUBLED, BRUCE noticed as he looked out the door.

"He was here!" Toby called from the other room.

Bruce moved through the officers to the kitchen. "Where?"

"He drove by the main house around three-thirty."

Bruce looked at the officer who had originally pulled him over. "We were still on the side of the highway at that time."

"He passes your house at three-forty, and again at four-ten headed back out toward the highway."

"Can you see her in the car?"

Toby shook his head. "No. Only him."

Bruce ran his hand over the back of his neck. "What if he dumped her here somewhere?"

Alex made a move to him again, but stopped short of grabbing him. "Don't talk like that," he shouted and then drew in a deep breath. "Sarah wouldn't let anything happen to her. She gets too much joy out of kicking the asses of men who do her wrong."

Bruce lifted his eyes to meet his friend's. There had been a shift in Alex in that moment. He knew the strength of his sister, and though perhaps, her abduction was because of her relationship with Bruce, he hadn't directly had anything to do with it. He knew Alex understood that now.

Toby handed an officer a piece of paper, and he and four more officers walked out of the house.

"What was that?" Bruce asked pulling out a chair and sitting down.

"His address from HR. I don't know if it's real or not, but it matches his ID," Toby confirmed as the officer, who had been coordinating everyone from the information Toby had given them, moved to the table.

Bruce looked at his watch. It had only been two hours since the officers had pulled him over. Two hours since Sarah went missing. Two hours he'd been holding his breath.

It seemed like an eternity he'd been standing in his kitchen with Toby at the helm pulling up the information they'd need to find this lunatic, and Alex paced impatiently waiting for news.

"We have search teams mobilized in the area. There is a creek nearby," the officer in charge said. "We have a helicopter headed our way for aerial search."

"The creek runs behind the property," Toby offered. "About a mile from here. It's accessible. I have a shed with kayaking gear on the creek's edge. They are welcome to the equipment, and have my permission to break into it if they need to search it."

The officer nodded. "I appreciate the help." He turned to leave, but Bruce stood and reached for him.

"What can I do? I can't sit here anymore and wait to hear something. I need to help."

The officer scanned a look over him. "You're her point of contact. She'll reach out to you or her brother if she finds a way, or she'll come here. We need you to man the house and your phones."

Bruce nodded. He hadn't expected much more.

He watched the lights on the cars as they pulled away from the house. The sun was beginning to make its descent behind the mountains Bruce had grown so fond of. Tonight though, he grew afraid of the dark.

CHAPTER 46

*S*arah moved against the walls, her hands finally gaining feeling. When she came to the paddles, she pulled one off of the rack.

It was then she could hear footsteps outside of the shed. Someone had come for them. Someone found them. She nearly dropped the paddles and ran toward the door, but she stopped herself.

There was only one set of footsteps outside. If it were a search party, there would have been many more. If she started to scream, he'd open that door and hurt her—hurt them both.

Instead, she moved herself back to the wall and walked silently toward the door. When he opened it, she would attack, and there would be no mercy.

But he didn't open the door. The footsteps continued around the shed and Sarah waited inside the door, the paddle lifted over her shoulder like a baseball bat ready to swing.

Then the smell of gasoline permeated her nose.

She couldn't keep silent now. "Let us out!" she screamed. "Let us out!"

She screamed when something hit the door, hands she thought as they pounded against the wood.

"You're going to die. You're both going to die!"

"This isn't about us! Let us out!" Sarah shouted.

"This is payback," his voice growled through the slats in the door. "He should lose just like I did."

Sarah pressed her hand to the door. "He lost too. He watched his mother die," she pleaded. "Don't go down the same road as his father. There's no reason."

The door pushed in toward her, still latched, and Sarah picked up the paddle again ready to fight. But the door never opened.

Her heart began to thud so loudly, she could hear it. "This isn't how he did it," she called out hoping to stop the man outside. The gasoline smell had begun to choke her. She had to assume he wasn't done. "If you're trying to be like Sam Bennett, you're doing it wrong."

Sarah gripped the paddle tighter.

The man pounded against the door again. "His method was sheer greed!" he shouted. "He raped and killed for fun. I'm killing for revenge." His voice was filled with a demonic rage.

"You killed Emily! She had nothing to do with Bruce!"

"It made you weaker. You are my ultimate conquest. And Mindy's death will hurt him too. And wait to see what I do to his grandmother. He needs to hurt." His voice growled through the door.

Sarah turned, still in total darkness, toward the person in the corner. Mindy.

"You can have me. Just open the door!" she shouted, her hands still wrapped tightly around the paddle.

The air around her shook. There was a helicopter. They were searching for them. It was almost over. He'd lost. She and Mindy were alive and they were going to walk out of that shed.

Sarah felt the tears begin to well in her eyes. They were going to be saved.

Her thoughts of freedom were halted when she heard the crackling sound that began at the door and quickly moved around the building. He had set the gasoline on fire.

~

THERE WAS SCRAMBLING AGAIN, AND BRUCE WATCHED AS THE officers hurried to their cars.

"What's going on?" Bruce thought the question, but it had come from Alex's mouth.

"The helicopter spotted movement at the shack, but now it's engulfed."

"On fire?" Alex asked, and Bruce was grateful, because he had stopped breathing and couldn't speak.

"Crews are on their way."

Alex turned to Bruce and grabbed his arm. "C'mon, we're going down."

Bruce stared at his dearest friend unable to move, but the officer stopped their progress.

"We still need you here," he said calmly.

Alex let go of Bruce and stood toe to toe with the officer. "That's my sister down there, if she's down there. I deserve to be there when she comes out."

"We don't know that anyone is down there. This could be a diversion."

Bruce let out the breath that had been held up in his lungs. "He's deviating from my dad's plan. I mean, he's not copycatting."

The officer focused on Bruce now. "What does that mean?"

Bruce shrugged. "He's causing a scene. My dad didn't do that, except to take someone from where he left someone. They're down there," he said looking the officer in the eye. "I can't tell you how I know that. I just feel it in my gut."

The fire trucks flew down the road outside the house and Bruce gripped the back of the chair.

Alex grabbed Bruce's arm again. "We're going."

The officer watched them as they passed and then took a call on his radio. Bruce didn't hear what was said, but the call had consumed the officer's attention.

Alex opened the passenger door and all but threw Bruce inside before he ran to the other side and climbed in.

"I'll be damned if they're going to hold us prisoner here and Sarah is down there fighting for her life," he growled and scanned a look over Bruce as he started the engine. "What's with you? You should be mad as hell. You should have been running to that damn shack the minute they realized there was a building was down there."

What was with him? Bruce was numb. The vision of seeing his mother fight for her life, her hands wrapped around his father's as she tried to fight off the knife played in his head. The blood. All the blood.

Bruce sucked in a breath.

"You were right to forbid me from getting involved with her," he said and he didn't even recognize his own voice. "This is because of me."

Alex put the car in reverse, kicking up gravel as he put it in drive and headed down the road. "This isn't the time for you to get sappy or stupid. You're a goddamned man in love with a woman and you should be there fighting for her."

"If I fight, I might not stop!" Bruce yelled, and he realized what he said, and at the volume in which it had come out. It was a revelation to himself. "If I let the anger take over, maybe I take a life, maybe I hurt her."

"Don't do this, man. Don't get all deep in your fricking head now."

"I love her. I love her so much it hurts. But you were right. She deserves better than me. I should never have fallen in love with her."

CHAPTER 47

*S*moke filled the space immediately, and the heat was quickly becoming unbearable.

Sarah got on her knees and crawled to Mindy. "We need to get you away from the walls," she said as she felt for her arms or legs.

When she'd found both of her ankles, she realized they were tied. This was going to hinder their escape, she thought.

Sarah took hold of Mindy and pulled her toward the center of the shack. It was then she heard the sirens and the cars. There was still hope. They were going to get out of there.

She scrambled to find the paddle again, and when she did, still on her knees, she pounded against the crackling wood.

"We're in here!" she screamed. "Get us out!"

There was too much noise to know if anyone heard her, but she didn't give up. She continued to scream and use the paddle, but the smoke was burning her lungs.

The sounds of the sirens changed and she knew the fire truck had arrived.

"Mindy, you keep breathing shallow and you hold on. They're

going to get us out of here. We're going to get you home to your family," Sarah promised.

The smoke changed, and she knew they'd started to get water on the fire, but it still sizzled around them. Then there was a thunderous noise at the door, and Sarah dropped down next to Mindy. It came again and again, until light broke through and a man stood in the doorway.

"Is there anyone in here?" he shouted.

"Yes!" Sarah coughed out the word and hoped the man heard it.

A moment later a bright light shined right on them and Sarah had to hold her hand up to it. It was blinding and she couldn't see anything.

"We're going to get you out. How many of you are there?" the man asked.

"Two, I think."

The smoke continued to change, and the lights grew brighter as the man walked toward them.

They were safe, she thought as the tears that had threatened since the moment the man attacked her in her new home began to fall.

She'd be in Bruce's arms in no time.

THE CAR BOUNCED ON THE DIRT ROAD AS ALEX SPED TOWARD THE blazing building in the distance. A moment later, he steered off the road and headed the car for the trees.

Bruce grabbed hold of the handle above his head. "What in the hell are you doing? You're going to kill us."

"No! I'm going to kill him!" Alex shouted as he raced toward a figure which ran in and out of the trees.

Bruce watched the headlights of the car bounce up and down,

and once in a while it would catch the man that ran against the bank of the creek.

"He had to have walked back in so we wouldn't have seen his car. Son-of-a-bitch isn't getting away from me."

Bruce watched as Alex's eyes went wild and the car moved faster.

Holding on tight, Bruce watched as the figure grew closer. In the lights he could see that it was Austin and his stomach clenched. He'd spent time with the man, and all the while he was aiming to hurt Bruce and those he loved.

The flash came out of nowhere and the windshield shattered. Bruce ducked and Alex slammed on the brakes.

When they both lifted their heads to look at the other, Bruce knew that neither of them had been hit.

Simultaneously, they both opened their doors and lunged from the car, taking off toward the figure that ran near the creek.

Alex, who had always been a faster runner, closed the gap. Austin turned and the gun glinted in the light from the car.

Bruce screamed for Alex to duck, which he did, as Austin let off another shot. But Alex was back on his feet in a moment and Bruce watched as he tackled Austin and they both went down.

Bruce continued to run toward them, another car now coming up from behind them, this time with flashing lights. But Bruce didn't stop. He had to get to Alex before Alex murdered a man.

As he grew closer, he could see Alex's fists flying into Austin's face. Austin's hands pushed against Alex, but there was no forgiveness. Alex was in that blinded mindset where he could kill the man. Bruce had seen it before.

Someone was running behind Bruce.

When Bruce reached Alex, he grabbed hold of him and pulled him from the man he straddled. Austin's face was bloodied and he coughed trying to catch his breath. The gun still gripped in his hand.

"What are you doing?" Alex screamed as he tried to free himself from Bruce's grip.

"You're going to kill him."

"Damn straight I am!" He shoved at Bruce again as two officers ran past them. "I'm not done with him!" Alex yelled as the officers rolled Austin over and cuffed his hands behind him.

"We've got him," one of the officers called back.

"I want my sister. Where is my sister?"

Austin spit blood, narrowly missing the officers shoe. "She's dead. They're both dead."

Alex began to charge at him again, but Bruce held him back.

"I'll kill you!" Alex shouted.

The officers dragged Austin to the car, and one of them turned back. "They're getting the women out of the building now. One of them isn't in good shape."

Alex turned to Bruce and shoved him to the ground. "You should have been right there helping me kill that bastard."

"And what would that have done but made us just like him. Just like my father. And wasn't that what you were afraid of in the first place?" Bruce argued as he got to his feet. "I won't have anyone's blood on my hands, and neither will you."

"You're a wuss."

"I am. I'm scared of my own shadow," Bruce admitted. "But Sarah is going to need you. You were right all along. I'm no good for her."

CHAPTER 48

*A*nother officer pulled up to them. "C'mon, I'll take you down to them. They're loading them into ambulances right now."

Alex moved to the car, but Bruce felt as if his feet had melted to the earth.

"Get in the damn car," Alex demanded.

"Just go. She needs you."

Alex moved to him, gripping him by the shoulders. "Get in the goddamned car."

"I left her in the house alone. She accused me of killing Emily and Mindy. There is no reason she wants to see me right now, or ever. Go. She needs her family."

Alex studied him. "I can't leave you here alone."

"I'm fine. I'll get back to the house and that's where I'll stay. I promise. I'm not going to run or do anything stupid. She just needs you now. She needs her brother."

Alex gave Bruce's shoulder a squeeze, then turned and climbed into the police car.

"TAKE HER FIRST," SARAH CRIED TO THE FIREFIGHTER THAT HELPED her to her feet. "Get her help."

"They'll get her," he confirmed as he wrapped her arm around his broad shoulders and helped her through the broken down door as more firefighters started toward them with a board to carry Mindy out.

Outside of the building, the air was thick, and the sun had gone down. Lights from the cars and trucks illuminated the small shack which still burned behind her.

The man who helped her, led her to an ambulance where two paramedics waited for her. They set her on the gurney, placed an oxygen mask on her face, and began to assess her condition.

Another car came flying toward them with lights flashing. When it stopped, her brother flew from the car and ran toward her.

Before he could even say anything to her, they both turned to watch them carry Mindy out on the board. The other set of paramedics met them a few feet from the building with the gurney. They began working on her right away, and Sarah began to cry.

That bastard tried to steal her from her family, and Sarah wasn't sure he hadn't succeed.

Alex turned his attention back to her. "You're okay? Did he hurt you?" he asked as he raised his hand to a cut on her face.

"I'm fine," she said through the mask before she lowered it. "I'm fine. I'm a little knocked around. But, Mindy…"

"They'll take care of her," Alex promised.

"He's gone. He'll come back," she said.

Alex shook his head. "I jumped his ass and beat him up," he smiled. "Bruce wouldn't let me actually kill the man, but…"

"Where is he?"

Her brother took a step back and ran his hands over his hair. "He's not coming."

Sarah batted her eyes as the tears welled. "Why?"

"He says I was right. I should have kept you away from him."

"No. You were wrong."

"Not my words, they're his. He said you accused him of killing Emily and Mindy and he left."

The tears were warm on her cheeks as they flowed. "I did do that. I accused him."

"He wouldn't hurt anyone," Alex defended him. "I know that now. God, he wouldn't even let me kill the man who tried to kill you."

"I love him."

"Then you're going to have to figure out how to tell him that. He's hurting over this. He knows he brought this on."

Sarah shook her head. "No. He didn't do this. This isn't his fault."

The paramedic put the mask back on her and eased her back as they lifted her into the ambulance.

She pulled down the mask again and looked up at the man who listened to her chest. "The other woman?"

"They're taking her to the hospital now. She's in bad condition."

"She's alive?"

The man nodded. "She's alive."

TOBY STOOD BEHIND THE BAR IN HIS BASEMENT AND STARED AT Bruce who rolled the bottle of beer Toby had handed him between his palms. They'd sat in silence for nearly an hour.

Austin Wilkes had been taken into custody, and the officer assured Bruce that he would never see the man again. They'd promised him the same when they'd taken his father away too.

Only this time he knew, he'd be in a court room to face the man, and so would Sarah, Mindy, and Emily's husband. It might be over for now, but it wasn't over forever.

And when would the next maniac come for him and those he loved?

His grandmother had agreed to stay with Ray and his family for the night, but she assured him there was no need to keep her from her home longer than that. She'd been looking over her shoulder since she began taking in foster children. Only the Lord was going to take her down, she'd promised him.

"You should go to the hospital and see her," Toby said as he sipped his water from the glass he'd poured himself. "Your wallowing is making me think less of you."

"I think less of me," Bruce admitted. "If ever there was reason to have my man card taken away it was today."

"I didn't really mean it. I was just kidding," Toby said walking around the bar and pulling out one of the stools to sit on.

"I'm serious. I shouldn't have walked out on her when she accused me like that. She didn't mean it and I knew it. And then when you even mentioned the shack, I should have just gone."

"I think an officer asked you to stay put."

"My heart should have told him to shove that idea up his ass," Bruce argued. "I pulled Alex off of that asshole. I should have been the one to tackle him and beat him. And when they took them out of the building, I should have been there, but I couldn't."

"This is a heavy thing to carry with you forever. You're going to need to figure this out."

"I know," Bruce finally took a sip of the now warm beer, then pushed it away. "What I know is I need to leave. I need to start somewhere else."

"Bullshit," Toby said shaking his head. "You need to stay here where your brothers are and your grandmother is. You need to stay here where the woman you love is."

"She needs to be free of me."

"Then let her make that decision. We're here to help you heal from this. Don't think you owe any of us enough that leaving is the right thing to do. We'd think less of you, trust me. You've always faced everything. The fact that we didn't even know what you were facing says that you're one strong S.O.B."

Bruce let out a breath. "I really appreciate that. Can I stay in the guest house a while longer?"

"Forever if you need to."

CHAPTER 49

The doctor shined the light in Sarah's eyes one more time before giving her a nod and walking out of the room.

Alex stood from the chair in the corner and walked toward her. "You look and smell like shit."

"I hate you," she said with a snarl.

"I don't believe you." He ran his hand over her hair, protectively, and studied her face.

She'd seen what she looked like. That creep hadn't gotten in too many licks, but she'd been thrown around enough she was bruised, dirty, and now stitched together.

"He's not coming, is he?" Sarah asked and watched her brother's lips tighten.

"No."

"This wasn't his fault."

"You can't convince him of that. That guy knew his real name. He knew everything about Bruce."

Sarah shook her head. "Still not his fault. And I shouldn't have accused him of being the one that killed Emily. I don't think I even meant it, but when I had Rachel's phone in my hand, and that voice came through before Bruce walked through the door," she let out a breath, "I lost my mind."

"Then give him some time to process it all," Alex sat on the edge of the bed. "He pulled me off that guy and wouldn't let me kill him. He didn't want me to carry that forever."

Sarah smiled. "See, it's not in him to hurt anyone."

Alex nodded. "I know that now."

"Talk to him for me, please," Sarah pleaded. "I don't blame him for this. Hell, I talked to the guy and never even thought to mention it to anyone."

"That guy made it so you wouldn't think a thing about it. He played you. He played Bruce and Toby too."

She took her brother's hand. "Just make sure Bruce knows I love him. I'll wait for him to come to me, but he needs to know."

"I will."

"And what about Mindy?" Sarah asked.

"She's really bad. They have her in good hands. She's getting IVs and they're taking care of her. There would have been no way she could have gotten out of there without you."

"And her husband?"

"He's on his way here, they said."

"I hope that guy fries for what he did to Emily, to Mindy, me, and what he did to Bruce. How do you get over this?"

Alex kissed Sarah's cheek. "You talk to Rachel, and then you keep talking to professionals that will help you deal with it. You're lucky to be alive, and you're lucky he wasn't a true copycat of Bruce's father."

She was grateful for that. Sarah had watched the documentary. The small cuts to her back and the bruises on her face weren't anything compared to what Sam Bennett did to the women he'd kidnapped.

Sarah understood now why Bruce had gone through what he had to ensure he didn't pass on his family genes.

Maybe she was wrong. Maybe she should go to him. But she'd

accused him of murder. How could she have done something so thoughtless? How could he forgive her for that?

Didn't time heal everything? Perhaps if she gave Bruce some space, he'd work through this with her and they could move forward, whatever that meant—and she didn't know.

One thing was for damn sure, she wasn't moving into that house she'd had built. She would turn around and sell it. But giving Bruce time meant she didn't have anywhere to call home.

Alex would let her stay with him, in the basement once occupied by Bruce. That much she was sure of.

When the door opened again to Sarah's room, an officer walked through the door, and there were two more that waited in the hallway.

"How are you doing?" he asked.

"I'm going to be okay. I have a lot of people to thank for getting me out of there."

The officer nodded. "Your brother and your friends were a great help in us finding you so quickly."

Sarah squeezed Alex's hand.

The officer stepped in closer. "I need to get some statements from you. Do you feel as if you could talk about all of this?"

Sarah nodded. "I'm ready. I know just how lucky I am. This is nothing compared to what it could have been."

"It's still quite a big deal, one he's going to pay for for a very long time," he assured her.

She hoped so. "Is it okay if my brother stays?"

The officer nodded as he pulled over the chair from the corner. "Of course. Whatever makes you more comfortable." He turned on the recorder on his phone, and took out a notebook. "If you don't mind, tell me everything you remember, and I'll ask some questions later."

Sarah closed her eyes for a moment, took in a long breath, and let it out slowly. This was going to be a norm, she thought.

She'd be asked to relive this over and over again so they could put the man away.

Her heart ached even more for Bruce now.

How many times had he had to relive his mother's murder just to have his father locked away?

CHAPTER 50

*S*arah untied her shoes and looked around the gym. Three Sundays had passed since her kidnapping and attack, and three weeks of basketball games they had played without Bruce.

Toby had allowed him to work from home, and he and Rachel had been the only ones to see Bruce. Rachel couldn't say much more than, "He's just not ready to face everyone yet," but Sarah wondered just how much more time he was going to need. Didn't he need everyone to heal? Didn't he need her?

She slipped on her sandals, tucked her basketball shoes into her bag, zipped it up, and stood as she lifted it onto her shoulder.

"What are your plans today?" Catherine asked her as she bounced Celia Rose on her hip, trying to keep her daughter from kicking her enlarged belly.

"I don't know. I think I need to go see him," Sarah said, realizing that was what she was thinking. "He needs to know he's not alone."

Catherine smiled. "I heard the guys saying they should all just show up. They think he's had enough time to collect himself."

"I guess all of us who love him are thinking the same thing."

"You still love him?" Catherine asked.

"I've always loved him. I don't think there's ever been anyone but him. From as far back as I can remember, there's always been something special between us."

Catherine rubbed her stomach. "Then you should go to him."

Sarah leaned in and kissed her niece on the top of the head. "I think that's what I'll do."

SARAH'S HEART RACED AS SHE DROVE AWAY FROM THE YMCA AND drove toward the guest house she'd shared with Bruce. As she passed by Toby's house, her breath quickened too. The thought that the last time she'd driven down that road, in that direction, she'd been in the floor of that man's car, her hands bound behind her back and her face bloody.

She needed to calm herself. This wasn't going to help Bruce.

Rachel had taught her how to relax and to breathe. She'd given her the name and number to a therapist that Sarah had started to see immediately. Seriously, if Rachel and Bruce could both live productive lives, so could she.

His car was parked out front, and Sarah pulled in next to it.

Her hands had gone damp just thinking about talking to him. What if he didn't want to see her? Could she handle that?

As she looked up through the windshield, she decided she'd better have it figured out, because there he stood on the front porch watching her in a T-shirt and jeans, his feet bare.

Sarah pushed open her car door and stepped out. She had never been nervous around the man a day in her life, so why was now so different?

"Who won the game?" Bruce asked casually.

Sarah tucked her hair behind her ear and closed the door to her car. "I'm not even sure," she admitted. "Probably Connor," she teased and Bruce chuckled as he took a step toward her.

"You look good," he said.

"Thanks." Did she bring up the scar on her back, or the fact that today was the first time she couldn't see the bruises on her face?

No, he didn't need to relive it either—even though he hadn't even seen her in those moments.

She took a breath, because she could feel the need to be angry about it rise in her chest. It wasn't worth it, she thought. He had his own demons.

Bruce cleared the last step to the porch and stopped, so she continued to walk toward him. "You need a haircut," she teased and he ran his fingers through his hair.

"I suppose I do."

"I miss you," she said, and then stopped walking. She hadn't meant to say that, but she couldn't help it. It was the truth.

Bruce tucked his hands into his pockets. "I've missed you too."

"Why haven't you reached out to me?"

Bruce shrugged. "There's a lot of weight on my shoulders. If I wasn't who I am, you wouldn't have gotten hurt, Emily would be alive, and Mindy wouldn't have been taken from her family."

So, he hadn't unpacked it all, yet, she decided.

"I don't blame you."

"I do. And I'm sure your brother does, too. After all, this is why you were forbidden to me."

Sarah moved closer to him, but leaving enough room, just in case one of them needed to retreat.

"I didn't know that's why he didn't want us together."

"And now that you know?"

Honesty, she reminded herself. She needed to speak what was in her heart. "Now nothing changes. I loved you before I knew. I love you now."

His eyes narrowed as if he were trying to find truth in her words. "You thought I had it in me to kill Emily."

They were words she could never take back. "I was scared."

"Because of me."

"Bruce, I love you."

"You need more time to heal. I think you'll change your mind."

She needed to close the gap. What if she touched him? Kissed him?

"I won't change my mind." Sarah reached her hands to his chest, only to have him capture her wrists and stop her from touching him.

"I need more time."

Sarah pulled back her hands. "How much time?"

"Because of my father I almost lost you. Alex almost lost you."

"Your father didn't do that."

"He caused it," he insisted. "I can't think about touching you, until I know I would never hurt you."

Her chest hurt with his words. How could he possibly think she wouldn't want to be with him? How could he turn her away like this?

"I don't know what to do," she said, her eyes welling with tears.

"Go home."

hursday guys' night had taken a back seat the past few weeks. It wasn't the same if they weren't all together, they had decided. But tonight, it wasn't just guys' night, or nachos and margaritas with the girls, this was going to be an intervention.

Sarah sat at Toby's bar next to Mrs. Griffin, who sipped from a glass of wine which Toby had assured her was from his private stash of a company he owned.

Charlotte and Connor sat on high stools at the Pac Man and Defender arcade games, while Ray and Kelly looked on. Catherine sat in a recliner with her feet propped up while Alex danced around the room with Celia Rose on his hip.

Rachel handed a sleeping Angela to Craig as she buttoned up her shirt after having fed the baby.

Toby walked around the bar so that he was in the center of the room. "So, what are we going to do? We're his family, and Bruce needs us."

Craig lifted the sleeping baby to his shoulder. "We just need to show up to that asshole's house and tell him to snap out of it."

After he said it, he turned toward Bruce's grandmother. "I'm so sorry, Mrs. Griffin."

She smiled. "He is being an asshole."

Sarah watched as Craig's shoulders relaxed.

Sarah looked around the room at the blank faces. "I say we just storm the house. He's going to be mad, but you are his brothers. His grandmother is right here. He's not going to run. He might fight."

Alex nodded. "The first one he'll come for is me."

Sarah shook her head. "He won't lift a finger. He's afraid to."

Bruce's grandmother drank down the wine in her glass, and then, as if she were still fifty-years-old, she hopped off the bar stool. "We're not getting anything done sitting here. He needs an ass-whooping to set him straight," she said. "He won't run off if I'm there."

Boosting Celia Rose up onto his other hip, Alex nodded. "That's why we brought you in. You're our big guns."

"He deserves his pity party, but that boy has never wanted to be his father, and he's not. He needs to be reminded of that. And you're all the ones to do that." She turned to Sarah. "You still love him?"

"Yes."

"You lost a lot. You gave up your new house. You were attacked. You have a scar that will make you remember that for the rest of your life. And you'll never have his children."

Sarah swallowed hard. "It doesn't change how I feel."

Mrs. Griffin nodded and turned her attention to Alex. "And you've had his back since you were eleven. Does that change now?"

"No," he was quick to answer, and it eased the tightness in Sarah's chest.

"Then he needs to know how much he's loved. That's what's going to set him free."

Bruce's grandmother started up the stairs before she turned back to Sarah. "You still have that thing I gave you?"

Sarah thought of the ring that still rode around in the center console of her car. "I do."

"Maybe you ought to think about using it," his grandmother said as she turned back around and climbed the stairs.

BRUCE DROPPED HIS FEET FROM THE CHAIR HE'D HAD THEM PROPPED up on outside on the back patio. There seemed to be a calming breeze that welcomed him there, and he'd been sitting there for nearly an hour.

He heard the sound of a car on the road and he knew by the time he walked through the house, they would be just pulling up in front of the house. But as he got to his feet, he decided that wasn't the sound of just one car.

Maybe he'd just sit back down and let the cavalry come to him.

He'd been expecting this ambush. It was time to face them all, he decided. Chances were there would be punches thrown, insults hurled, and feelings hurt. There was no guarantee that they'd emerge as friends when it was over.

When he opened the front door, he saw the cars. There was one for each of his friends. What he hadn't expected was the number of people that would climb out of those cars. They had brought their entire families, including children. Okay, that was low. There was no way he was going to punch Alex if Celia Rose was around, and especially if Connor and Charlotte were there to watch.

When the back door of Alex's car opened and he helped Bruce's grandmother out, he knew he was the losing party to this fight. They'd brought her to talk him out of the house.

"I don't think you're playing fair bringing my grandmother to fight your fight," he said as they all began to converge onto the front porch.

"I didn't say I was coming to play clean," Alex said as he took Bruce's grandmother's arm and helped her up the steps.

His grandmother looked at him, reached for his cheeks as she would when he was younger. With her hands on his face, she lowered him so she could look him in the eye. "Let's go out back and sit for a bit. These kids have things they'd like to talk about."

She dropped her grip and walked past him into the house.

Bruce shook his head. He might as well follow. He'd already lost whatever fight he had within him.

CHAPTER 52

*B*ruce helped his grandmother into a chair as everyone piled around them on the back porch.

He watched as Kelly walked down the steps with her kids toward the creek. Well, at least they weren't going to be watching Bruce's fall. That made him feel only slightly better.

"We've decided it's time you come out of your house and we face what happened—together," Alex began.

"You've all decided."

"Yeah. You seem to be taking your sweet ass time, and we don't want to wait anymore."

Bruce nodded. "So my dealing with this is an inconvenience to you all?"

"It makes basketball games uneven."

Bruce shook his head. "That's just bullshit."

His grandmother swatted her hand at his arm. "You don't talk back to them."

He heard Toby snicker.

"I'm not ready."

Rachel took a step toward him. "We think you are. We all miss you. It's not basketball games. It's Thursday nights. It's time with your friends. It's starting something new with Sarah."

"That's over."

Alex moved to him until they were toe to toe. "Just like that? You get to make the call on that?"

"You don't want me with her."

"I didn't want you with her. There's a big difference."

Bruce crossed his arms in front of him. "So now that I got her best friend killed, my ex-girlfriend kidnapped and nearly killed, and Sarah kidnapped..." he didn't want to finish the sentence. "Now you're okay with it?"

Alex mimicked his stance. "You didn't do that. Austin Wilkes did that."

Bruce cringed just hearing the name. "She will forever look over her shoulder with me."

"I don't think she will. Besides, I trust you."

"Why?"

Alex placed his hands on Bruce's shoulders. "You didn't let me kill him."

There was a compassion in Alex's eyes, one Bruce hadn't seen since Alex had found out about his relationship with Sarah.

"You would have."

Alex nodded. "Of course I would have. Look what he's done to you."

Bruce swallowed hard. "You're thinking about me?"

"We all are. Man, you aren't your father. You've done everything to prevent yourself from ever being him. Why don't you let that shine now? We all love you—you asshole."

There was a collective laugh among his friends and even his grandmother.

Bruce looked around at the faces of his friends, their wives, and their children. His grandmother reached for his hand and gave it a squeeze.

But they weren't all there, were they?

"I can't help but notice Sarah didn't join your crusade."

"I'M HERE," SARAH SAID FROM THE DOORWAY.

Craig and Ray parted so she could walk between them.

Bruce and her brother stood toe to toe.

Alex took a step back as she walked toward Bruce. "They needed to tell you how they felt."

"I guess that's what they did."

"These are your brothers. They have your back."

Bruce nodded as he chewed his bottom lip. "And you?"

"I told you. I love you and miss you." She gathered his hands in hers, and this time, he didn't pull away. "Bruce, I don't want to live my life without you. You are compassionate, kind, loving, and fun. My whole world has always revolved around you, and what happened to all of us doesn't change how I feel. I feel safe with you."

Sarah took a breath and looked at their joined hands.

"I can never take back the words I said that hurt you. I can only hope that in time, you can forgive me for them," she offered as she lifted her eyes to meet his.

"You had every right to say them."

"No, I didn't. Because you're not that man. You're all those other things I said, and have always believed. Please, please, say you still love me."

Bruce raised his hand to her cheek, and she trembled under his touch. "I've never loved anyone else, not the way I love you."

"Can we go back to us? I mean, can we make the life we were planning?"

BRUCE LOOKED AT ALL OF THE PEOPLE WHO SURROUNDED THEM who knew every one of his dark secrets now. They had come to save him, he realized in that moment. They had come as a unit to share with him their love and their support.

He looked back at Sarah, who stood next to him with worry in her eyes. Hadn't he waited his entire life for a love like they had?

He thought back to their first kiss at New Year's and the mystery of it. When he had told Ray he was living out a life-long fantasy by kissing Sarah, that hadn't been an embellishment.

And now here she was asking for him to do the one thing he'd already always done—to love her.

Bruce took her hands again and kissed her fingers. "I'm sorry I put you through this."

"We're all processing it in different ways. But we need to all process it together."

He nodded. "I do love you. I do want what we had before."

Sarah drew in a deep breath and let it out. "Thank goodness."

Bruce watched as she exchanged glances with his grandmother and then tucked her hand into her pocket.

Before she showed him what she had, she got down on one knee before him.

"What are you doing?" he asked and then looked around the room at the faces that looked as quizzical as his did. Well, all of them except his grandmother, who smiled wide.

"Bruce, there's only been you. Every crush. Every fantasy. Everything I ever wanted was you." She opened her hand to reveal the ring he was more than familiar with. "Will you marry me?"

He hadn't expected it. Wasn't he the one that was supposed to be on his knee, holding out a ring?

Bruce blinked and then again.

Sarah curled her hand around the ring again and held it tight in her grip. "You're freaking me out."

"I just wasn't prepared for this."

"Your grandmother gave me your grandfather's ring to give to you and ask you to marry me. So maybe you could give me an answer?"

Bruce lowered to one knee, his hand still in hers. "Will you marry me?"

Sarah lifted an eyebrow. "You're answering my question with a question?"

"I guess I am."

She blew out a breath. "I'll marry you."

"And I'd like nothing better than to marry you."

EPILOGUE

The July Fourth celebration at Alex's had been abruptly canceled when Catherine had gone into labor. Sarah had rushed over to take Celia Rose, and now she and Bruce sat on the back porch of the guest house with her niece and watched the sky for sparks of color that might make it high enough to shine over the tops of the trees.

Celia Rose's eyes had begun to close as Sarah rocked her in the chair. Obviously, looking up at the sky was something you appreciated when you grew older. She amused herself with the thought.

When Bruce's phone rang, he looked down at the ID then slid his finger over the screen and turned on the speaker.

"You have news for us?" he asked, knowing it was Alex on the other end of the phone.

"We have another little girl," his voice beamed through the phone. "God, I'm surrounded by women."

"Serves you right," Sarah took the jab at her brother in good fun. "I can't wait to meet her. What's her name?"

"Gretchen, after Grandma," he said, and Sarah wiped away the tear that had appeared in her eye.

"I love it. Congratulations."

"Will you both come by tomorrow and bring Celia Rose to meet her?"

"Of course."

They ended their call and sat in silence for a moment. Celia Rose opened her eyes and smiled up at Sarah, then moved so that she wrapped her arms around Sarah's neck, then rested her head on her shoulder.

"She's going to be a fantastic sister," Sarah said, rubbing her niece's back.

"Just like her auntie."

"You know. This little one is my world. And I know Gretchen will be too."

"You look natural like that," Bruce said, and when Sarah looked in his direction, he was grinning at her.

"Like what?"

"With a baby in your arms."

She adjusted Celia Rose so that they were both more comfortable. "That's very nice of you to say, but…"

"No buts. I know I can't give you a baby of my own, but I still think we should have one."

"I think we have a lot of time to think about it."

"I don't know. I'm already in my thirties, and you're right behind me."

"Years behind you," she reminded him.

"I want you to know, I think we'd be good parents. I've come a long way," he admitted. "And every day, I think I have something to offer to a kid like me."

"Like you?"

"Yeah, someone who needs a family, just like I did. I can't imagine my life without my grandparents. They absolutely changed my life."

"I think your grandmother would argue that you changed theirs too."

"And there is the blessing in adopting. Though, you deserve to have your own baby."

Sarah nodded. "And Toby has offered, but that creeps me out."

The sentiment made Bruce laugh. "Me too."

"I'll keep it in mind though." Sarah reached for his hand and they intertwined fingers.

"My grandmother called again today and asked for a wedding date. She reminds me each time she's not getting any younger either."

Sarah nodded. "I put in a call to that wedding planner."

"You're sure you don't want to elope?"

"I need elegant and extravagant. I'm only doing this once."

Bruce laughed. "How elegant and extravagant?"

"Very." She laughed as she continued to rub her niece's back. "I'll get back to you on a date."

Bruce stood and took the sleeping baby from Sarah, then reached his hand down to help her from the chair.

"You know, just because we're not going to have kids the normal way, doesn't mean we can't practice like we were trying."

Sarah stopped, pulling back on his hand. "I am not doing that while my niece is here."

"Okay then. Let's just pretend we're teenagers babysitting. We'll put her to bed and make out on the couch."

Sarah laughed. "My brother has forbidden me to date you," she said playfully.

"All the more reason I want to kiss you."

SOMETHING NEW

We hope you enjoyed book one in the Funerals and Weddings
Series, *Something New.*
Please enjoy an excerpt from the final
book in the series,
Something New.

Sometimes love shows up when you've stopped looking.

FUNERALS AND WEDDINGS SERIES, BOOK 5

Something
NEW

BERNADETTE MARIE
BESTSELLING AUTHOR OF THE DEVEREAUX FAMILY SERIES

SOMETHING NEW

*M*usic echoed through the empty house. Speakers wired in every room played the same song. With one voice command, Toby Maxwell could change the song, the volume, or the location of the music. He'd had the technology long before the rest of the world.

He had never found the need to use it to drown out the sound of the chaos in his own head before. Work had done that for him. His business had been his mistress for nearly a decade. The large house had been his trophy.

Now it all felt empty—the house and the job.

He hated when he got in his own head. But ever since his company had been infiltrated by a murderer, and his friends hurt, Toby couldn't help but feel that pang of guilt, and it mixed with the isolation and loneliness.

Turning on the lights to the kitchen, Toby opened the subzero refrigerator and pulled out a bottle of water. He scanned a look over the empty shelves, which could hold platters of food. It would do him good to entertain again, but he hadn't wanted anyone in his space.

Closing the refrigerator door, Toby sat at one of the stools that circled the large island. There was no clutter on the counters like there was at Alex's house. The small kitchen in the Denver bungalow now served four, as Alex and his wife Catherine had brought home two babies in less than a year. It wasn't as quaint as Kelly and Ray's kitchen with drawings attached to the refrigerator door, drawn by their children.

Rachel and Craig's kitchen boasted a high-chair too.

The guest house a mile down the road, where Sarah and Bruce were still living, had a rustic kitchen which Toby had picked out when he'd remodeled the guest house. It, too, was quaint and cozy for a couple just starting out together.

But his own professional grade kitchen was cold and lonely, just like the house with enough rooms to house all his friends.

His life had been quiet two years ago, before Coach Diaz died and he was reunited with his brothers from college. Since then, they'd been as tight as any family could be. Only now, the other four were married or engaged. Three of them had families. But, much like when they lived in the dorms and Ray had Craig and Alex had Bruce, Toby lived alone.

He gave the command for the music to stop, and the silence was deafening. Pulling his phone from his pocket, he started a group text to the men who had once been known as *the fabulous five*, as Coach Diaz had designated them.

It's been a long time since we did guys' night on a Thursday. What do you say? Tomorrow night? My house? Wings and beer?

Toby sat in the silence and waited for answers.

Craig was the first. *Rachel says I'll be there.* He'd added a laughing emoji. *I miss you all.*

They'd all been together continuously since Coach's funeral, until Sarah had been kidnapped by a man who had worked for Toby and was copycatting Bruce's father's killing spree.

He blew out a breath. They'd all needed a break from everything and everyone once that was over.

Bruce was the next to chime in. *Wouldn't miss it for the world.*

Ray added, *I'll be there, and the kids want to come too. Anyone have a problem with that?*

They all agreed that it was fine as Alex sent his reply. *I'll bring Celia Rose. Catherine could use a break with only one baby for a night.*

And just like that, his brothers would be together again.

Feeling a little relief, Toby stood and walked out of the kitchen, leaving the light on for comfort.

As he walked through the living room, he saw a white car turn down his road, and then stop just beyond the drive.

His heart began to hammer in his chest. He could kill the next reporter that come looking for Sarah and Bruce after her kidnapping.

When the woman raised her phone to take a picture of his house, Toby headed for the front door.

LAURA SNAPPED HER PICTURE AND LOOKED DOWN AT HER PHONE TO see that she'd captured the essence with the sun going down behind the grand house. If only she could get an invitation inside, she could take her business to the next level. She just knew it.

"I don't know who the hell you think you are, but get the hell off my property," a man bolted from the front door and headed in her direction.

"I'm sorry," Laura stammered as she backed toward her car. "I didn't mean…"

"I don't need any reporters sticking their nose in our business."

Gripping tightly to her phone, Laura lifted her head and pushed back her shoulders. "I'm not a reporter, sir." She pulled a card from her suit jacket and handed it to him. "I'm a bridal consultant. Laura Torres," she offered as she held out her hand to shake his, but he didn't respond to that, so she pulled it back.

The man narrowed his eyes on her. "You're lost."

"No, sir. I love your house." She willed her heart to calm, and gripped her phone tighter so her hands wouldn't shake. "I think it would be an amazing venue for weddings."

"You're working with Sarah?"

Laura shook her head. "No, sir. I don't know Sarah, though if she's a bride-to-be, please give her my card."

She was sure he'd growled at her. "My house is not for rent or for show. You can take your fancy car and your fancy suit and go."

He turned back toward the house and Laura bit down on her bottom lip.

"Again, I'm sorry, sir. Have a nice evening," she called out, but he didn't respond.

Laura watched him disappear into the house and slam the front door closed. That hadn't gone the way she'd hoped. And, if that was the owner of the house, he certainly wasn't who she thought he was. In her research, she'd found the owner of the house was one Toby Maxwell, thirty-five, and the owner of one of the biggest tech companies in Boulder. That man didn't look like the pictures of the well-educated, multi-millionaire, philanthropist. Maybe that man had been Toby Maxwell's evil twin.

PLEASE REVIEW

We hope you enjoyed Something Forbidden by Bernadette Marie. If you did, we would ask that you please rate and review this title. Every review helps our authors.

Rate and Review: Something Forbidden

5 Prince Publishing
Arvada, Colorado, USA

MEET THE AUTHOR

Bestselling Author Bernadette Marie is known for building families readers want to be part of. Her series The Keller Family has graced bestseller charts since its release in 2011. Since then she has authored and published over forty-five books. The married mother of five sons promises romances with a Happily Ever After always... and says she can write it because she lives it.

Obsessed with the art of writing and the business of publishing, chronic entrepreneur Bernadette Marie established her own publishing house, 5 Prince Publishing, in 2011 to bring her own work to market as well as offer an opportunity for fresh voices in fiction to find a home as well.

When not immersed in the writing/publishing world, Bernadette Marie can be found spending time with her family, traveling, and running multiple businesses. An avid martial artist, Bernadette Marie is a second degree black belt in Tang Soo Do, and loves Tai Chi. She is a retired hockey mom, a lover of a good stout craft beer, and might have an unhealthy addiction to chocolate.